The River Gods

BRIAN KITELEY

The River Gods

FC2

TUSCALOOSA

The University of Alabama Press
Tuscaloosa, Alabama 35487-0380

Published by FC2, an imprint of the University of Alabama Press, with support provided by Florida State University, the Publications Unit of the Department of English at Illinois State University, and the School of Arts and Sciences, University of Houston–Victoria

Address all editorial inquiries to: Fiction Collective Two, University of Houston–Victoria, School of Arts and Sciences, Victoria, TX 77901-5731

⊗

The paper on which this book is printed meets the minimum requirements of American National Standard for Information Sciences—Permanence of Paper for Printed Library Materials, ANSI Z39.48–1984

Library of Congress Cataloging-in-Publication Data
Kiteley, Brian.
 The river gods / Brian Kiteley. — 1st ed.
  p. cm.
 ISBN-13: 978-1-57366-151-5 (pbk. : alk. paper)
 ISBN-10: 1-57366-151-1 (pbk. : alk. paper)
 1. Massachusetts—History—Fiction. 2. Northampton (Mass.)—History—Fiction. I. Title.
 PS3561.I855R58 2009
 813'.54—dc22

                    2009010731

Book Design: Steve Halle and Tara Reeser
Cover Design: Lou Robinson
Typeface: Garamond
Produced and printed in the United States of America

My dear Brown...I have a habitual feeling of my real life having past, and that I am leading a posthumous exis-tence.

—from John Keats's last letter

I've known rivers:
Ancient, dusky rivers.

My soul has grown deep like the rivers.
—Langston Hughes

The tree is smoother than we expect—the limbs at this height, about fifteen feet off the ground, are worn by something, an animal, a disease, weather? We manipulate our bodies, her back, my shoulder, her elbow, to reach a level of comfort and organization. Her parents are inside eating their TV dinners. The light from the television bathes our naked parts in blue. As we begin, there is a flash from the TV, the scene has shifted, and the brightness startles us. She grips a smaller branch just then, which makes us sway and heightens the tension of our contact, the reverberating tree swinging inside our bodies.

The next night, close to dawn, I ride my Harley Electra Glide up Elm Street just before Child's Park, coming back from T.J.'s, where we had a keg in the woods, a dry run for the festivities tomorrow, after graduation. The turn onto Woodlawn is always tricky. Drivers wanting to pull out can't see you coming around the curve, and I know I'm going too fast. The curious thing is I *can* see around a corner and down Woodlawn to her bedroom window, and I know she's lying in bed wearing the *John Barleycorn* tee shirt I gave her two years ago and no underwear. The station wagon comes into view, turning left on Elm Street, and I can tell a bad thing will happen, not necessarily to me, but to the three little kids in the back seat. What are they all doing up at two in the morning? I veer and slide. Thank God I'm wearing the helmet and leather chaps my father gave me. It'll be a bad burn, but at least they won't have to take skin from my ass to replace missing skin on the thigh. The slide is clean. I find I can hold the handgrips so the front wheel points slightly downward, which makes for a small gap my leg fits under.

While I'm noting this, the station wagon drives in slow motion across Elm into the little triangular park by the high school. The father must be drunk, because he speeds up and plows into a fifty-foot-tall pine tree. The sound is a cartoon-like *blam*. My body comes free of the bike and I do a nice roll, as if escaping oncoming linebackers. The end of my roll has me standing upright, dusting off my chaps, which show no skid marks. I see the kids slumped forward in the back seat of the station wagon, and one has fallen out of the car onto the grass. I break into a run, a tight button-hook, but something like a very large needle jabs me in the chest. I fall. Life leaps athletically out of me. The kid on the grass wakes to see blood gush from my mouth, me on my knees. Somehow I can see that I've broken a rib and the sheer dumb luck of running so hard has sent the splinter of bone into my heart. "He died instantly," I hear the ambulance driver tell the father, who isn't drunk after all. Or else my death has sobered him up quick.

Standing there, I watch these kids grow into manhood. It all happens too fast to narrate, but I witness their lives unfold and fall apart. They feel responsible for my death, except it's only the father's fault. Three beers and six bourbons at the backyard barbecue that went on way too long. They were the last to leave, their hosts giving them the evil eye, his kids asleep in the car for hours while his wife tried desperately to get him to leave. The father dies of drink, but not dramatically. I watch the liver grow gray, laced with more and more hard veins of dead tissue. He's sixty-seven when he goes—I have to wait as long as the living for the future to arrive.

My name is Israel Williams and I am confined to a log jail in Northampton for a treasonous letter I wrote to an English supplier. I suffer from palsy, so my son Israel puts these words on paper for me. My wife Sarah died in her sleep three years ago, and much of the disastrous rebellion against the King I have witnessed since then has not made the sense it would have made were she in her chair next to the beehive oven. I freely admit I addressed the letter, of which I am convicted, to an English ship resting in New York Harbor, but this was only to achieve communication with a regular supplier of our shop in Hatfield. At that time, I surmised this war would soon be won by the King. Now the tide has turned. I am not a traitor. Nor am I Monarch of Hampshire County, as I was once called. The phrase "River God" should be retired. I prefer to apply it to my late cousin, Jonathan Edwards, or to his grandfather, Solomon Stoddard. It was juvenile of me to ride past

Parson Edwards' house off King Street so often, without once paying him a courtesy visit. Sarah frequently urged me to make amends, but the pleasure of the snub was too great.

The mob rule that incites this wicked rebellion annuls those elements of justice our people do have in their favor. I once opposed the Crown's pine laws that saved for Royal Navy ship masts the tallest white pines, which we in the colonies wanted to fashion joists and studs out of for meeting houses. I do not lament any other earlier opinions. The mob made us run in circles on the town green, while my daughter Eunice lay dying in Pittsfield. I signed an agreement I do regret, but it was under duress. Because of my infirmities I now consult my ease, and I do not foresee the day I will walk up the steps of the old Hatfield home. I wish I believed in ghosts, for then I might have tangible evidence of my wife. I will not hurry this life on, but I am eager to catch up with Sarah beyond, hear the news, listen to her wisdom and sense of restraint, and be told where my shoes and my pipe are.

July 1962
Jean Kiteley, 33
Mother of Barbara, Brian,
and Geoffrey, wife of Murray,
daughter of Em and Joe

I am no longer so shy and out of my depth in ritzy western Massachusetts. We drove up from New Jersey (where my parents live), at the end of our cross-country trek from San Jose. The view of the Pioneer Valley when we passed Mt. Tom and Mt. Holyoke was breathtaking and hopeful. We sold our house on Dent Avenue in San Jose and will not buy a new one until we learn the lay of the land. It has been a surprisingly cool July. We moved into the Smith College faculty apartments on Fort Hill Terrace, a large horseshoe-shaped set of one- and two-story buildings. My husband, Murray, will teach philosophy at Smith College in the fall. There are over a dozen families at Fort Hill, mostly new faculty, from all across the country. Everyone welcomed us with open arms, but I worry this is too easy, an uncharacteristic experience in what I know is usually stuffy, cold-shouldered, aristocratic New England.

But the parties! The flirting! Every Saturday night since we arrived someone sets up a kiddie pool of ice and beer. We pass jug wine from Dixie cup to Dixie cup. Someone cooks hot dogs and hamburgers—or exotic shish kabobs—on a grill built into the central picnic area. Adults swing drunkenly on the swings—or make themselves sick on the merry-go-round. There is laughter. At least on Saturday night, no one's marriage seems rocky. The children's bedroom windows are always in earshot. Most of the children are under the age of ten, which makes things easier. The infants are quiet and contented, perhaps because they can hear us laughing, shouting, telling bawdy jokes nearby.

Northampton won me over almost immediately—against my better judgment. The town appeals to me a great deal, but I don't want to be hurt by it. Murray cheerfully encourages me to make friends—with women or men, he truly does not care—and I believe him. So I try to ask questions, understand the knotty problems these men—and some of their wives— wrestle with. We are used to the college life, after three years at San Jose State, but there is a quality to the questions here, poking, prodding, asking for ever more amplification. Murray is thrilled. It's as if I am listening to myself answer questions from above my body. One of our nearest neighbors, Robert Golden, seems to love talking with me. He is a kind man. He genuinely loves his wife Grace, who is moving more quickly than the rest of us into middle age. Grace has a sixteen-year-old son who is off at a Jewish camp in the Catskills. Robert is telling me about the history of the town. His area is American history. He's written a famous book, and Murray says he is likely to be snapped up by the Ivy Leagues any day now.

I try to pay attention to Robert's story—something about a man named Joseph Hawley and his uncle Jonathan Edwards, whose church we're now attending. Halfway across the wide play area, Hugh Cowell, a sociologist, is hectoring his wife Anna again, telling her and several other wives how he needs six hours alone in the study off the living room to do his work. Impossible, with two infant girls bumping into furniture ten feet away. Murray never needs alone time, but he is always alone in his mind, working out difficulties that in spoken English sound like another language. Hugh Cowell is in many ways a dear, even if he is a bit intimidating, but the way he and Anna argue—well, I imagine their sex life is satisfying. This thought makes me color, and, even in the dark, Robert notes this. He asks if I am feeling well. Behind this question is the next logical question, "Are you pregnant?" Robert has four children and he is rooting for us to catch up with them. No thanks, Robert. The implication of this unstated question makes me blush fiercely—and I decide I truly love this town. I tell Robert what I was thinking about Hugh and Anna, and Robert, bless his heart, laughs as loudly as anyone has ever laughed at something I said. This causes several satellite couples and singles to wander near to hear what was so funny. Life cannot, for the moment, be any more pleasurable.

We came here for Gold, not God. The Moors drove Spain and Portugal west to look for new trade routes to the Indies and China, so Spain and Portugal divided the New World, with the complicity of the Popes. The discovery of all the Gold in the southern Americas, but not here, drove down the price of Gold in Europe, Bankrupting our treasuries, which were already devastated by the Black Death. The fall in the value of Gold (and I might say God) had the unforeseen Benefit of wiping out much of the Ottoman's wealth in the Near East. The Sultan still pounded at Europe's back gate, but it was clear the Turks would not be able to pay their soldiers long or buy land out from under us. The Kingdoms of Spain and Portugal mismanaged their trade, killing off or expelling their best tradesmen, the Arabs and the Jews. The Dutch and the British, both seafaring Protestant nations, ended Catholic Spain's pretense of ruling the Old World, the New World, and the Next

World. Every once in a while, an English sailor was captured and trapped in the machinery of their Inquisition. When one English sailor escaped and reported the horrors to London, we redoubled our efforts against the Papists.

Here are some of the religious sects in London at the moment: Papists, Brownists, Calvinists, Lutherans, Family of Love, Mahometans, Adamites, Brightanists, Armenians, Sosinians, Thessalonians, Anabaptists, Separatists, Chaldæns, Electrians, Donatists, Persians, Antinomeans, Assyrians, Macedonians, Heathens, Panonians, Saturnians, Junonians, Bacchanalians, and Damassians.

In Virginia, the Gold they discovered was Tobacco, nearly as valuable. I confess to finding its taste vile. Farther north, in New Holland, we tempted Fate. Furs, lumber, potatoes, and dried fish were all we could trade in—meager profit. I was there for the Establishment of Fort Good Hope—later called Hartford. I happened to be along for the Founding of Agawam, which Pynchon renamed Springfield. To be at the end of another Civilization pleases me in my old age. The idea of the town preceded the fact of the town. Pynchon and his partners sold the land of Nonotuck out from under these Indians. There were 300 Indians and perhaps 100 Warriors among that number. The deed:

> All the said Premises the said Pynchon & his Assigns shall have & enjoy Absolutely & clearly forever, all Incumbrances from any Indians or their Cornfields. In Witness of these present the said Indians have Subscribed their marks this twenty-fourth day of September, 1653.

Pequahalent, Nanassahalent, Chickwallop, Nassicohee, Skittomp.

I will enjoy Nonotuck absolutely but not Forever.

The fifth graders play marbles every day after school. The South Street School is two blocks from home at Fort Hill. Geoffrey and I walk home most days hand in hand. Geoffrey is in third grade, I am in second. Some days our mother meets us at the crosswalk. Other days she does not. I want to play marbles with the big kids, and every day I bring my own small bag of marbles as an offering. They never let me in the game. Geoffrey and I sit or stand outside the circle and watch. One day, a big kid brings a new marble. He unveils it carefully from his pocket. It is the biggest marble I have ever seen, perfectly clear, with a flat spot. Someone says, "No fair. That's for a sofa." But the other boys allow this giant into the ring. I watch helplessly. At one point the marble comes rolling (with a limp) toward me, and I do what seems most natural. I pick it up. I run. When I come to the crosswalk my beautiful mother is waiting at the other side, my baby sister standing very still. My mother waves. The crossing guard escorts me across. My mother gives me a small hug, and my sister says nothing, though she looks hard at my fist, which barely covers the marble. The three of us walk home.

Geoffrey arrives a few minutes later. He is old enough to cross, with the crossing guard, without our mother on the other side of the street. I lie on the bottom bunk of our bunk bed, staring at the marble, which I press into my pillow. Geoffrey enters the bedroom casually, hanging his jacket on the peg, examining a book on his little desk, writing something on a piece of pink construction paper. Finally he comes over to the bed. He asks me what I will do tomorrow. I haven't thought about that. I imagine going back to the school, the big kids following me down the halls just two paces behind, right up to the door of my classroom. I imagine them standing there all through class, just staring at me. Geoffrey says he will take the marble back to school right now, and there probably won't be any harm. With tears in my eyes, I hold the marble against my chest and let the marble roll from my hand into my brother's hand. Geoffrey walks into the kitchen—I follow—and Geoffrey tells our mother he is going back to school. Our mother says, "Hmmm," but no more. She is making dinner, a wonderful casserole with potato chips on top. I stay to smell the dinner, but I also watch out the window, as my brother walks with maddening deliberation past the deep drain that goes so far down no one knows where it comes out.

ŗ

Location filming for *Who's Afraid of Virginia Woolf?* started last week. I did a run-through outside the house we were going to use as George and Martha's place. It was on the corner of the Smith College campus, a few dozen yards from the waterfall at the end of this aptly named Paradise Pond. I realized quickly that the waterfall noise was going to drown out the one scene we really needed in Northampton, so I asked the dean of the college, who was just hanging out around the edges of the setup for the shot (the actors weren't even in town yet), if he could do anything. He said, "Sure. I'll just have them turn it off." Turn off a waterfall. It was done the next day.

I graduated from the University of Chicago, so this east-coast J.D. Salinger world of debutantes and faded aristocrats made me nervous. I am thirty-four years old. I have directed a few plays on Broadway, and I had a fairly successful run as a comedian on stage and television with my dear girl Elaine May. This is a new world for me, but I have to say the prospect of directing Elizabeth Taylor and Richard Burton did not disconcert me as much as dealing with these effete eastern snobs at Smith College. The couple turned out to be pussy cats—or teddy bears. None expected what they saw of Elizabeth the night of the first shoot. She wasn't even in the scene, but she came, in costume, in her blowsy makeup that took five or six tries to get right, thirty pounds heavier than she'd been in her last movie. She is a darling. I worked her hard, but she rarely lost her temper with me. Burton took most of the heat from her, and occasionally poor Sandy Dennis, god knows why. Liz was giving me a joking hard time for suspending the shoot the day before to go down to Manhattan for a lunch with Jackie Kennedy. We were closing in on two years since the assassination, not that I'm admitting anything untoward was going on in New York.

Liz and Dick and I went for a walk later that night, maybe one or two in the morning—who looks at a watch in the midst of these hectic shoots? I was scouting out more locations for a similar walk they would take coming back from a party at the beginning of the movie. I liked the lay of the campus, the odor of a noxious gingko tree near the college president's house. I wanted to be able to include that smell in the movie, at the very least as a throwaway line. It surprised me, at some point, surrounded by these beautiful homes and tall elms, that I was so casually out for a stroll with Elizabeth Taylor and Richard Burton in a small town in western Massachusetts. Of course, we did not see a soul on the streets. Imagine their surprise if they had run into us. We passed a bottle of champagne back and forth. Liz requested two cases of the stuff, $800 worth, for her dressing room. She seemed perpetually amused that these outrageous demands were met. Dick reminded her he was tenth in box-office drawing power last year, and she was eleventh. They are not what I would call a real couple, but who am I to speak, running off to New York for a ridiculous rendezvous with the widow of a president.

We turned onto Massasoit Street. "That red-baiting strikebuster Coolidge lived here," Liz said. Dick told me that his wife was much better read than him in terms of politics and world events, but she had a shameful ignorance of Shakespeare. "The dear girl had never read *The Winter's Tale* or *Measure for Measure* when we met. Can you imagine an actress not knowing the greatest female parts in the language?" Liz cackled and threw the champagne bottle into the street, with a fair sidearmed delivery, clearly hoping it would break. It skidded across the pavement, spilling expensive liquid in a long arc, but then it simply clinked against the opposite curb. "You stupid cow," Dick said, in character, but maybe not. "Now we have to walk all the way back to the fucking hotel for another drink." Liz turned, laughing, toward me, but she gave a vicious punch at Dick's midsection. He doubled over, laughing even more riotously than she had been laughing, but Liz steamed off down the street, as if she were going to walk back to the hotel, except she was heading the wrong way. Dick kneeled on the grass, gasping for breath and genuinely worrying me. When he had enough breath, he called out to his wife. "Wrong direction, you idiot." Liz let out a scream we were becoming accustomed to in rehearsals, but it still put my hair on end. Dick said, "Look. You can see her thinking out her complexities even as she plays them. So touching the girl wants to learn how to act."

Lights came on in several nearby homes. I hoped a taxi would magically appear, but we were in a town that rolled up its sidewalks at six in the evening. A silver-haired fellow appeared out of the shadows, on the walk to his house. He asked Elizabeth Taylor, in a voice loud enough for us to hear, if everything was alright. I expected her to cry rape, accusing us both with the unbridled fury she seemed capable of at a moment's notice. But they had a quiet chat, and Liz walked the man up to his home, where they seemed engaged in a perfectly ordinary, human communication, as if she hadn't been the most beautiful woman on the planet as recently as six months before.

My teacher is doing numbers and letters on the blackboard when the principal knocks on the classroom door. This is not normal. The principal stands outside the door, her head bent, her blond hair covering her face. She is not young, but she is not old either. She makes a strange set of noises. One of the other students whispers, "She's crying." The teacher excuses herself and walks down the hall with the principal. It takes a long time for anyone to come back to the classroom. By the time someone does come back—another teacher we do not know well, a big man—the room is rowdy. This does not bother the male teacher, which surprises the class into silence. His eyes are red and at one point he wipes his sleeve across his nose. He is crying, too. He says, "School is dismissed. You can all go home. The president has been shot and killed in Dallas, Texas." Then he leaves the doorway, and no one in the classroom moves.

A boy stands and says, "Well, I'm going to the playground." He stomps out of the room. It takes many other students leaving before I go—I am still worried about the big kids who played marbles. When I do leave, I look down the hall at a knot of teachers. They all stand very close together, as if they are hugging each other. The sound that comes from them is a soft chuffing noise. Static scritches from somewhere, quiet radio voices interrupting the static every few seconds.

I look for Geoffrey, but I can't find him. I want to be home, so I run. To my surprise, the principal is the crossing guard at South Street. I walk over the crosswalk, careful to avoid the solid white bars, and then I run as fast as I can to the apartment. Today is the day our cleaning lady Mrs. Kennedy comes. I ask her every week if she is the president's mother, and every week she laughs—I like asking the same questions again and again.

Mrs. Kennedy is a big woman, with very white skin and gray hair tied up but spilling over its knot. She wears a dress that makes crinkling noises. She smells like my Play-Doh, after I left it outside one night. She lives in a long row of houses. Each house looks exactly the same as the other houses. When she sees me slip into the kitchen, her first words are, "What are you doing home now, young man? Are you playing hooky?" I do not know what that word means. I say, "The President has been shot and killed in Dallas, Texas." Mrs. Kennedy, who is only a foot away, reaches down. I think she is going to hug me, but she slaps me hard on the cheek. I burst into tears, pride terribly injured, amazed at how mean Mrs. Kennedy is, but also fascinated, in the midst of my sobbing, that something *I* said made her upset.

Geoffrey walks slowly into the kitchen just then. He says, "Turn on the radio, Mrs. Kennedy. It's true. The president is dead." Mrs. Kennedy is big enough that she can gather both of us into her arms and carry us into the living room. She does. She collapses onto the couch. Geoffrey returns to the kitchen and a moment later brings her a glass of water. He's even put ice cubes in it. I stand watching Mrs. Kennedy cry for a long time. Her crying immediately stops my own tears. Then I go over to the television to see what's on. I rarely get to watch television this time of day. Every channel has grown men looking gloomy and sad, talking very slowly, turning to other men in chairs next to them to ask complicated questions. There is no *Swabby the Sailor Man* or *Leave It to Beaver* or cartoons. Mrs. Kennedy makes me stop changing channels when I come to Walter Cronkite. I start sniffling at something about this man's voice. Geoffrey leads me by the hand to my bed. He says, "It is very sad. But don't worry, there is a person who will become the new president. Our teachers are sad because the president who died comes from this state. Now you get some sleep, just lay your head down. If you have any questions, call me. The next few months will be difficult but we will pull through."

JFK was boasting about the White House operators. They could track down anyone anywhere in the world in half an hour. My wife, Tony, and I were neighbors of the Kennedys in '58 and '59. Tony's ex-brother-in-law was high up in the CIA now, and he had an odd fascination with Truman Capote, so we happened to know Capote was up in Northampton, Massachusetts visiting an old boyfriend who taught at Smith. Tony threw out Truman's name. I had interviewed him once for *Newsweek* when I was stationed in Paris. He was sharp as a tack, I'll grant him that. JFK called the operator, and not ten minutes later she called back. Kennedy chatted for a while, cradling the phone on the crook of his shoulder as if he were talking with an old friend, leaning casually against a low secretary table. Tony and Jackie exchanged glances. JFK was impervious to the squeals of delight on the other end of the line. He told Capote a story of campaigning in western Massachusetts for his

Senate re-election. Larry O'Brien had taken him to Northampton to see an old Irish politician. He said the three of them had a few at Rahar's, where the ex-mayor said Calvin Coolidge ate lunch every day. Capote seemed to interrupt the president's story because Kennedy said, "What? Well, I'm wearing a gray sweater unbuttoned over a blue shirt, but no pants." JFK held the phone away from his ear for loud remonstrations we could not make out. "That's what I said. I am not wearing any pants. Jackie's modeling a bustier, even if there is precious little to boost. And two secret service agents are averting their eyes." Capote laughed long and hard, as we all did, and when the president rang off, he said, "I think I've got that vote sewn up." JFK straightened his back, and for an instant, I saw a spasm of pain ruin his handsome features. Tony, quicker on the uptake than me, said, "Can we get you something?" JFK's face resumed its mask of geniality. He said, "Naw. I'm on six medications, excluding the highball I'm about to order."

On the fifth of November, 1805, a Northampton resident found a riderless saddled horse and began a search for its owner. Marcus Lyon's body was found in the Mill River a short distance from the Boston Post Road, a bullet in his ribs and his head smashed to a pulp. Laertes Fuller, a thirteen-year-old boy, said he had seen two men in the area who looked like sailors heading toward New York. A sheriff's posse finally located two men not far from Mt. Vernon, New York, arrested them, and took them back to jail in Northampton.

The Irish defendants were not allowed to see their own lawyers until two days before trial. The one-day trial lasted until shortly before ten in the evening. Judge Sedgwick referred to Laertes Fuller and made this charge to the jurors: "If you believe the witness, you must return a verdict of conviction." The boy's testimony may have been believable, but it had no bearing on the crime and it was the only evidence presented in the case. Within minutes the jury found the two Irishmen guilty, and Sedgwick sentenced them to be hanged and their bodies to be dissected and anatomized.

The prisoners summoned a Father Cheverus from Boston. The Catholic priest went to Northampton to be with the two men in their last days. He was refused lodging in Pomeroy's Tavern. The wife of the proprietor said she could not sleep a wink under the same roof with a Catholic priest. Father Cheverus eventually found a bed at the house of Joseph Clarke. On the day of the execution, Father Cheverus preached in the town meeting-house, despite quite valid attempts by local ministers to prevent him from speaking. They feared riots. But they removed the windows of the building so the mob outside could hear. Father Cheverus' sermon was from 1 John 3:15, "Whosoever hateth his brother is a murderer." To the women present he said, "I blush for you; your eyes are full of murder." The women left in horror, but I am happy to report that more than 15,000 people witnessed the deaths of Dominic Daley and James Halligan. Northampton at the moment had 2,500 souls. I too witnessed the last kicks and moans, surprised by the restraint of these heathens.

I am close to my own death now, years later. My nephew Laertes Fuller had no knowledge of my act. No one did. I thought I would take to my grave the strange pleasure this murder brought me, the brilliant and colorful release of demons the adze clouting his head caused in my vision, however briefly. Watching Daley and Halligan hang did not take me off course. I was unmoved by their courage. I knew I had murdered Marcus Lyons and yet it seemed proper for these two ruffians to suffer. Still, I confess to the crime now, in a whisper. I wish to take credit for the one great act of my life.

Three stepsons, 16, 18, 19, and their father, 56, who teaches government at Smith College, and his second wife—the five of them mount the barricades, each in love with the second wife, even the second wife.

I am Isabelle, the second wife. In my short skirt I self-consciously climb the barricade made of café tables, chairs, and torn-up paving stones. I walk over the uneven surface with such grace and skill that all who watch me stop whatever they're doing. I love being the center of attention under these circumstances—a revolution "not unlike the 1848 Revolution," my charmingly pedantic husband says. At least he used to be charming. I also mourn this street in the Latin Quarter the way it used to be, when I was a junior at Smith College, eight years ago. History did not interfere with life in 1960. And prices were lower.

"He has disappeared into history," I overheard someone saying of the man I married. I also recall a Frenchwoman last night calling my husband virile, except the tart pronounced it "viral," which the boys repeated, out of their father's hearing, the rest of the evening.

I love being adored by my four men. When I married Larry, the boys were five years younger, their mother still in Northampton. When the ex-wife moved to Boston, things got better. But now the boys are older, more *viral.* I resist them as much as I can, but they look more and more attractive, much more attractive than their father, who in five short years has aged a great deal. The youngest boy is clearly homosexual. He may not know it. He sang a line from a beautiful Dylan song in a perfect imitation of Dylan's twang, just before they all retired to their rooms. He has his own room, as per Daddy's stern instructions. Does Larry know too? The line from Dylan is, "Don't the brakeman look good, Mama, flagging down the Double E?" This sounds suspiciously like longing, and I can almost get inside my stepson's mind to imagine the picture he has of this brakeman, which is not all that different from a fantasy I might have. I want to share these fantasies with the boy, but I don't know what he knows. Was I ever that young?

I know the boys spy on me in Northampton. I aid them whenever I can, partly to educate them, partly for my own delicious and illicit pleasure. In the flat we've been renting the last four months, it is much easier to spy. The two older boys and my husband and I share an adjoining bathroom. One barges in without the code knock. I am in the tub, under a layer of foam, but I sit upright in mock indignation to give him a full look—trouble boiling under the milky surface of this tub of defeated bubbles.

JULY 1962
JEAN KITELEY, 33
FORT HILL

In the middle of the night, I can't sleep. I check the boys and then Barbie. I go to heat up some milk. It sounds as if the party is still going on outside, but when I look I see only two ghostly figures—the moonlight playing tricks—strolling arm in arm toward the mansion at the far end of the open space where Barbie will go to pre-school. I make myself hot milk, grating a bit of nutmeg as my husband does, and I carry the mug out to the porch. The couple is still in the same place, moving in the same direction, as if they have turned around and come back to this one spot by the swing set.

I sit on the low cement wall, lift my legs up and over the wall, and find myself walking toward this couple. I don't recognize them from the apartments. Perhaps they are neighbors up South Street a way. I consider calling out, but voices carry so well over this flat playing field to all 19 apartments in the complex. I don't want to wake anyone. I sip my milk. It dawns on me very slowly that I am barefoot. The thought of stepping on glass or sharp rock enters my mind, but my body keeps walking. The couple ambles into a mist ahead and they are gone. I stop. I finish my milk and set the mug on the ground. I hitch my pajama bottoms up and take a path that goes into the woods and sinks down to a marshy area. Eventually the path will come out by the First National Supermarket. I feel my way slowly downhill. I'm told the marsh freezes in the winter and part of it is cleared for skating. At the end of winter, skunk cabbages give off a foul smell. I don't know how I know this.

Ahead on the path is a set of shiny, moving parts, brightened by the moonlight. When I come closer, I see arms and legs and bottoms. It is four or five naked children. One of them looks remarkably like my son Brian. I once caught him in San Jose playing doctor with a handful of the neighborhood girls—they were all lying flat, side by side and naked, in the little playhouse. But this can't be Brian. I saw him just minutes ago, sound asleep, covers thrown off. I come close to the children. They are like salamanders in mud. This is obscene, yet it also looks like play. The beautiful, lithe bodies hypnotize me. One girl looks up at me, with a strange smile on her face—I want to call it a *wry smile*, but that seems too adult a phrase for this beatific child. Another girl, near this smiling one, opens her mouth, and I smell a skunk, suddenly quite close by. The girl's open mouth lets out a deep, raspy voice, which says, "We enjoy our sin." I feel myself fall the way one does in sleep, and I have to sit down on wet heavy mud. I stand up, the mud cold on my thighs and bottom. I wipe off what I can. I say to the children, "Behave yourselves, I beg of you," and I walk away.

My mug's in the spot I left it. I climb over the low cement wall on my patio, exactly as I did at the beginning of this journey. I find another pair of pajama bottoms in the hall closet, and I put the soiled ones in the washing machine. I do not start the machine, because it will make too much noise, and I want evidence of this in the morning. I make myself another hot milk. I sit on the long couch Brian once covered with the contents of a large NIVEA Creme jar—he said he was icing a cake. I finish a mystery Murray is reading, starting at the place he dog-eared. I don't read the first fifty-seven pages, but I read with perfect understanding from there on. Slowly dawn comes, creating shadows and color where there were none before.

Murray is the first to greet the morning. "Were you up all night?" he asks. I nod, now terribly tired. Was it a dream? I check the washing machine—the mud's still there—and the boys' room. Brian is fast asleep, one leg over the lower bunk bed, snoring lightly. Geoffrey, propped up on his pillow, stares down at me as he often does, with that remarkable combination of childishness and philosophical gravity that both intimidates and delights me. "Is everything alright, Mother," the eight-year-old asks. "You looked in on us at three in the morning, did you know?" I smile and depart the room without answering. I crawl into my marriage bed and fall asleep instantly.

The situation of the Puritan soul, despite its outward security, is precarious. We uprooted ourselves from England and then Holland not to discover our identity but to protect it. We cast off the Anglican slave of Rome in England. Here our farms are rich, and the river valley is bright and open, but we sit on the edge of howling woods, within whose shadows Indians and devils play. At the final judgment, the Puritan must stand alone. The settlers gave little mind to the plan of the streets, which were laid out by cows. The first inhabitants built houses wherever these animals made a path. The land was from the beginning a savage antagonist. We pursued an immediate knowledge of the land to make it ours, but the complexity of this environment often killed or maddened us. We did not intend to stay in New England. Only our cows did. This was supposed to be a temporary sojourn, until England welcomed us back with open arms. But we are here to stay and we are corrupted by this unworldly beauty. Learning has brought disobedience, heresy, and sects into the world, and printing has spread all this out into the air like spores from a puffball, family *Lycoperdaceae*.

MAY 1968
GEORGE COWLEY, 16
PARIS, FRANCE

I follow my stepmother Isabelle up the barricade—piles of
café tables, wicker chairs, a metal food-storage cabinet, all ob-
viously "liberated" from cafés and bars nearby. My stepmother's beautiful legs, unclothed by nylon or stockings, are visible
up to her underpants because this new short skirt is hiked up.
A French student—he can't be much older than me, but he
says he helped erect these barricades last night so he has the
seriousness of a middle-aged man—takes Isabelle by the hand,
helping her over the hump, and kissing the same hand. He is
in love with her instantly, as we all are, even me, and you'll find
that I do not usually fall for such gaudy baubles.

My father and brothers are excellent bullies. I mean that each
is uncaring, didactic, appalled at the very slight hints of my ef-
feminacy, but they do love me, and more important they love
whatever they pursue with intellectual and physical—almost

rough-handed—vigor.

My brothers love football but hate baseball. Tennis is a faggy sport, but cross-country has a manly masochism. They love Eliot, Yeats is queer—you get the drift of their thinking. They're clearly not uneducated, but they do march to a military beat. Our own mother suffers from a masculine sense of order— her Germanic background—and, over the years, a hardening of the silhouette. They despise our father for not following through on the vows of his marriage, but they admire his choice of Isabelle, who cannily keeps them at a good distance. She allows only me into the inner circle.

We are taken to a restaurant that has been completely cleared of furniture. Another student tells us it will be safe here, but my brothers can't believe there is any real danger outside, and they want to see the Jeu de Paume before it closes (not realizing the general strike has shut everything down). I know all these things because I read the *Herald Tribune*. They insult me for burying my head in the paper to keep up with my Cardinals, who will make it to the World Series again. I've never lived in St. Louis. I root for them perversely, because they are not the Red Sox or the Yankees.

There is a moment when it does feel like some Second World War scene—dissidents and foreigners being rounded up for deportation to the camps. But the students return and break into the restaurant's walk-in fridge and pull out dozens of bottles of champagne, which my brothers hate—nothing but a red table wine for them. We sweep out into the street, nearly everyone with his own champagne bottle, my father noting what good vintages these are. The police begin to charge. This changes everything. Someone shouts *"Matraques,"* and most know, except my little family, what this means. I tell them it is a kind of billy club. We run down a narrow alley, a mistake, but we are lucky. We mostly stay on the Île Saint-Louis after that, crying from time to time because of the general atmosphere of tear gas.

I lie in my room, studying my older brother's bed. My bed is a mess. A baseball glove and a whiffle ball are somewhere in the folds of the covers. I look at Geoffrey's neatly made bed, a book on the pillow. The window is open and a summer breeze gently billows the light-green curtains. We moved into this house at the end of last summer, so we have not experienced a true summer here. School ended the previous Thursday. I will be nine years old in three months. Geoff is already ten and downstairs talking in his adult voice with Grandma Elsie and Grampa Eric. They are visiting this week. Elsie laughs every so often, each time saying, "Oh, Geoffrey." I crawl off the bed, and I twist one ankle against the buried whiffle ball. I jump to the floor, dancing and swearing, which I have only recently learned how to do. Geoffrey has not taught me how to swear, so I don't say the word in front of my brother, in case I'm pronouncing it incorrectly. When the pain subsides, I pick up the book from my brother's bed and read a sentence at random from the middle of the story: "Tom Swift knew the machine would fly only with the proper loving care." I see the words, and fortunately there is a picture on the opposite page of the mesmerizing flying machine that looks like a giant bathtub, but I can't make out the complex operations of every word, so I throw down the book, hissing under my breath the most maddening of words, a word Geoffrey often uses lately: "proper." "Brian, are you coming?" my brother calls from the base of the stairs. I say, "No, I'm not coming on your stupid bug collecting." Then I can't think of the proper word, and I slam the door. By instinct, I fall to the floor, pressing my good ear to the wood so I can hear the conversation in the kitchen below. "He's going through a phase," Geoffrey says to our grandparents. "He'll grow out of it."

The screen door bounces, and through the gauzy curtains I watch my beloved grandfather walking into the side yard with his butterfly net. My hand flaps in greeting. I want to know what my brother and grandfather say to each other when they go out beetle collecting. I go downstairs and twist the difficult front door knob. Steve Hemminger is playing in his back yard, across the street, an obstacle and temptation—I can see the shiny flash of the new Matchbox Corvette Steve got for his birthday. I close the front door almost all the way and run to the sidewalk. I look left and right. The block is unusually quiet. At the Dryads Green end of the street, one of the white sweeping nets flashes.

They turn left. With a sinking feeling I know where they're headed: the Mill River, a wild forest walk that I have not yet explored on my own. On the other side of the river is the insane asylum.

I look up at the house, such a big building, and I see my mother pass her bedroom window, holding her hair as if it were a cat, a brush in the other hand. She is about to do her hair the way she does it before going out for the evening, but it is ten in the morning. I want to know where my parents were going. I let out a yell that Steve Hemminger hears. Eric and Geoffrey are getting away. I wave off Steve and start to run. I run hard until the Stoddard house, where Jimmy lives. He is one of the bullies of the street, so I slow my pace and begin whistling. At Dryads Green I break into a run again. I come to the woods at the end of Paradise Road, stop at the beginning of the path, spy my grandfather downhill peering into his net.

I hang back. Eric takes out the thingy—a word I can never remember—aspirin? It frustrates me to have so much trouble forming words when they just flow past my brother's lips. Eric puts one end of the *aspatater* in his mouth, off to the side, the way my father sometimes smokes a cigarette, thoughtfully, distracted, when he is beyond answering questions no matter how often you ask them. With the other end of this doohickey, he taps against some small beetle, to make it let go of the net. Grampa Eric sucks on the one end of the aspirator—that was the word, but just as soon as I form it I forget it—shit! Eric sucks and the beetle floats gently into the old plastic bottle. This sucking of a beetle into a bottle profoundly disturbs me. I see a stump ten yards into the woods and realize I need a rest. Spying is hard work. I know which direction Geoffrey will go—away from civilization and the college campus where Daddy works. Geoffrey always goes toward difficulty, into abstract worlds I don't want to go. I sit down and my mind empties. I slump over and close my eyes, just for a second.

AUGUST 1813

JAMES GRAY, 20

A FATAL ACCIDENT

On a Sunday afternoon, Mr. Roach, Mr. Buchannan, and I were caught in a thunderstorm at the fish traps below the small dam on the Mill River. We took shelter at the root of a large tree. While we waited in palpable safety for the clouds to pass by, the tree was struck by lightning. Electric fluid descended upon us, killing myself and Buchannan, who was barkeeper to Mr. Buffington, and doing great violence to Mr. Roach. Mr. Roach and I were apprentices to Mr. Hull. My hat was torn to pieces, my eyebrows and hair greatly singed—and my coat much torn. Buchannan and I were thrown off fully extended, several feet from the tree, with marks of considerable violence on our heads and bodies. It seems that the electric fluid reached the hips of Buchannan and myself and from there jumped to Roach, for he was only affected in his lower extremities; his left thigh was a good deal injured, but not so much as his right thigh, leg, and foot—his pantaloons were torn to pieces, in the fore part, and the marks of violence correspond to the rent of them; his right shoe was much torn and his foot wounded, probably from the violent effort of the fluid to escape and the reaction of the shoe upon the foot when torn. In his pocket, Mr. Buchannan had three pieces of money, which were completely fused. Mr. Roach said I tried to speak, amid the lightning strike. He said a blue light seeped from my mouth, as if it were smoke, but it was denser than smoke, crackling, almost like handwriting.

I awake with a start, forgetting for a minute where I am. The color of the forest by the Mill River looks darker and bluer. I walk carefully to the path. Yes, I'm looking for my grandfather and my brother, who are collecting beetles down here so far away from my home. I hear the awful laugh of a sixth grader that says *I know things you can't possibly know.* Three boys come tearing down the dirt road from the wilderness end, laughing, throwing things, breaking off branches. One of them is Jimmy Stoddard, the Harrison Avenue bully. I freeze. I can't run, because these boys are bigger and faster than me and also headed in the only direction available to me. I can't see my grandfather or my brother—oh how I suddenly miss my brother, who usually talks Jimmy out of whatever he is about to do. I decide to stand very still. They move closer and closer. It becomes obvious that somehow they do not see me—this is too good to be true. Unless they are pretending not to see me till the last second. They run, they shout, Jimmy even skips once or twice—something he makes fun of in other boys. I realize I have stopped breathing for some time. It seems like a perfectly natural thing to do, not at all painful. The sixth graders give no indication of noting my presence. One is in danger of colliding with me. The three big kids swish past me, missing my scrunched-in shoulders by a hair. I swing around, expelling a big laugh-filled breath. I shout, "Can't catch me!" The boys do not break stride.

They have not seen me. I *am* invisible. I laugh again. I continue along the old river road, whistling. The sun has come out again. Pretty patches of shadow and bright sunshine on the Mill River look inviting. Fish leap here and there. Way down the path, where the river curves toward the baby dam, I see my brother sweeping a narrow section of grass with his butterfly net. I start to call out, but there is no point giving myself away after all this hard work. Ahead on the road a short distance, I notice a man standing with arms folded. The man looks odd. He wears a long gray coat. It is a warm June day. The coat is wrong for the weather but also just wrong—it looks old-fashioned but new. The man ordinarily would frighten me. He might be an inmate escaped from the insane asylum up the hill on the other side of the river, but crazy people wear pajamas. This man looks dressed for a costume ball or for one of my mother's Gilbert and Sullivan musicals. The sight of my grandfather and Geoffrey in the distance makes me feel safe. I start skipping toward the stranger, who seems to see me perfectly well. When I come up beside him, the man says, "Halt. Why do you trespass on my mill?" I stop, a little scared. I ask what trespass means. The man tells me he owns this land. I say, "Nobody owns the Mill River." I try to walk slowly around him, but a hand clutches my neck and lifts me off the ground. I can't even speak. The man carries me off into the woods.

We finally come upon a wooden building that reminds me of the old shacks at Sturbridge Village, where women in old-timey costumes make rock candy and men hammer red-hot horseshoes on anvils. The man in the long coat sits me down on a bench inside this cabin. I can now easily escape out the door— is this a trick? The man turns his attention to a metal bowl that sits on three legs atop a big fire. A fire in the summer? Is this man camping? Is he allowed to do that? This set of strange mysteries keeps my interest. The man stirs the pot and a powerful fishy smell is released in the room.

After this long silence, the man finally says, "This is salmon chowder. Salmon are the noblest fish taken in fresh waters. They are ameliorated by being three or four days out of water, if kept from heat and the moon, which has a much more injurious effect on them than the sun. I netted these in the Connecticut River. Where are your parents?" I say Harrison Avenue. "Where is Harrison Avenue?" the man asks. "Off Elm Street, between Kensington and Washington," I say. I love maps and know the lay of my world, as far away as Round Hill and the high school. The man says, "There is no such street as Harrison Avenue. The only street near Washington Street is Paradise Road. Perhaps you are thinking of Franklin Street, across Elm Street. But a little boy such as yourself should not cross the Northampton Street Railroad tracks." I look hard at the man. It is not that I have not heard what he said—no Harrison Avenue, a railroad running right through Northampton, if I am following this man's thoughts. But these ideas are so far beyond possibility that in the end I choose not to make sense of them. I also decide it is time to return to the river path. I stand. The man says, quietly, "Please stay a moment longer. My wife died in childbirth, along with my son. I make leather straps for horse bridles, but I am becoming indifferent to my business and my standing in this town. I have a house on Washington Street. My name is Rowley. I am planning to leave this region. A homestead in Illinois is being offered to Northampton residents, and I have heard that there are no trees on the plains. I have become oppressed by these great oaks and chestnuts and elms. They are God's greatest creations other than man, but the sun does not penetrate this forest floor here. My wife and I will depart at the end of the month."

I enjoyed this rambling talk, full of more mysteries, but I notice one mistake in the man's story. "You told me your wife died," I say. The man stirs his soup violently, banging the long wooden spoon, but he does not reply. Fish heads lie on a stump, their eyes looking right at me, milky and questioning. Mr. Rowley follows my gaze, and he scoops up the fish heads. He throws them into the pot. Eventually my stomach settles, and I stand. I say, "My grandfather is waiting for me. I hope you like Illinois. I was born in Minnesota, but all I remember is a very green backyard and those screaming bugs. What do you call them, chickadees?" The man continues to stare. It is not polite to stare. I make a little head bob, but it does not break the man's concentration. I step out the door and walk slowly along the path, my neck feeling wiggly.

I come to the end of the path and turn to look back. I sort of like the memory of this stranger. I liked his stories. But I see no cabin and no path. I say to myself, "I must have been walking longer than I realized." I continue toward the sunlit clearing.

When I come out of forest, I see Geoffrey and Grampa sitting on a long log. They are eating Grandma's sandwiches. Grampa moves to make room. He breaks off half a sandwich and hands it to me. My stomach growls in response. We all laugh. It is a beautiful summer morning, and everything is right in the world.

MAY 1874

GEORGE CHANEY, 40

THE WILLIAMSBURG FLOOD

I was overseer of the Mill River Reservoir, and I noticed the great smiling crack in the west side of the dam. I jumped on my horse and rode down to Williamsburg with the news, a distance of three miles. From there, other riders carried the word to Haydenville, Leeds, and Florence. The majority of people who worked and lived near the river escaped to higher ground, but 145 perished. A ten-foot wall of water swept everything along—people, houses, bridges, factories, trees, animals—all packed into a great mass of ruin. Witnesses say one man rode the flat roof of his small cabin about a mile downstream. He seemed unperturbed by the headlong rush—he sang at the top of his lungs, but no one could make out the words. His life was taken at the large bridge that collapsed his home and himself in one mighty boom, before the bridge itself disintegrated. Bricks acted as if with minds of their own, forming eddies, separate streams, and gnashing pools of bright red. Some thought they looked like salmon in their suicidal spawning runs upriver, when the waters turn the color of blood. Bricks left on the banks of the river created a nearly perfect road bed, except at steep angles. A fifteen-foot-tall metal wheel with fearsome teeth, used in the cotton mill in Williamsburg, rolled down the nearly solid river for miles, jumping over obstructions, at one point flying fifty feet in the air. It came to rest in a meadow eight miles from the original dam, and it lay there some twenty years as an unofficial memorial to the flood, before forest surrounded it and obscured its status.

MAY 1738

MEDAD STODDARD, 16

My uncle Jonathan Edwards and I arrived at the Connecticut
River ferry before noon. The ferryman asked if we would join
him in his midday repast. He had not eaten at all that morning—a spat with the good lady of his house—so he was too
hungry to wait on lunch. Pastor Edwards nodded yes, although
he was lost in thought. Inflamed by passion for my eighteen-
year-old cousin in Hadley, I looked on the scene with tender
excitement. Cascades of purple, white, and pink flowers flut-
tered in the breeze over the riverbank, and petals floated downstream. I watched the ferryman chew his lunch without teeth.
Here was one of the great majority of the town who could not
take the covenant because he did not own land. These men
waited outside the church after the sermons for notes written
down during the service. Edwards was oblivious of this fellow,
and in no way discomfited by this fellow's exclusion from the
church. I spoke several sympathetic words to the ferryman, but

I forgot what I'd said the instant the words left my lips. The hot sun and sweet air and drone of bees made us all sleepy. On the other side of the river, we could see Stephen Williams and his daughter waiting. Williams had the reins strapped tightly across the horse's breast—a cruel way of leaving the animal at rest; the tension of the man multiplies in the horse. I forgave him this moment of anger—and loved my cousin with this wash of river between us.

I sit in the armored limousine waiting for my daughter Julie to descend from her apartment in Northampton, Massachusetts. It is early May. Julie's husband, David, is "boning up" for a final exam. Julie is apparently better organized in her studies at Smith College. I enjoy my son-in-law's nervousness around me, which mirrors exactly my own, years ago, around David's grandfather, Dwight Eisenhower. Massachusetts is enemy territory, but I feel magnanimous, relaxed even. The smell of lilacs does not irritate my nasal passages as much as it used to do. Out of the gloom, a boy walks fearfully toward the limousine. Agents have closed off access to this intersection. The young teenager has short hair and good posture. The Secret Service agent tells me the kid's buying a present down the street for a girlfriend. "Not my girlfriend," the boy says. "My sister." I chuckle at this small act of bravery. I learn his name, Geoffrey Kiteley, and that he was a supporter of Lyndon Johnson even after he dropped out of the race. I tell him he's a smart kid, but the boy disagrees: "I have come to believe I don't know the world as well as I thought I did a year ago. Why, for example, do you continue to wage this unwinnable war when you said you had a secret plan to end it?" I suppress the warble of anger in my voice and try to change the subject: "Do you go to church?" "For a little while longer," Geoffrey says. The boy describes his church-founder's fondness for George Fox, who established the Society of Friends, nominally my own church. I opened this can of worms, but I have a policy of never talking to the world about Mother's churchgoing, unless it's on the campaign trail and thus impersonalized. Conversation about the Quakers verges on invasion of privacy, involving as it does details about childhood, and a humiliating sense of intimacy and loss (Mother's great love, my brother, died in that period). I surreptitiously press the button to roll up the window into which this boy is staring. The boy does not move a muscle for a moment, and I regret the decision, but I can't go back in time and undo it. Finally, the boy turns half away from the limousine, as if about to walk off. But he surprises me when he knocks on the window and does not wait for it to lower to speak again: "I hope you enjoy dinner with your daughter. And maybe you could give more thought to ending the American involvement in the Vietnam War."

MAY 1738
MEDAD STODDARD, 16

Molly Williams breathes up at me. Her breath smells of God. Neither Reverend Edwards nor Reverend Williams suspects us of evil. The two intimidating figures fall into conversation and ride ahead on horseback. We stay behind to check the bridles of the draft horse and to load the shipment of books from New Haven Jonathan Edwards is delivering to his cousin, Molly's father. In plain sight of the ferryman, with her back turned to him, Molly reveals one white breast to me. Quickly as she undid, she does up the blouse and jumps onto the buckboard unassisted. The ferryman sees this, with delight and scorn mixed equally, and it is the sort of thing he might report to her father, so she says, "A spider on the ground did throw me into fright." He nods. I presume he knows otherwise to be truth, but the ferryman would also have to admit he has nothing solid to report, for if he does it would include the subjective and salacious finding that Molly jumped onto the buckboard sensually, as if in a dance, as if possessed briefly by the Devil's own sense of play.

Molly and I do not deceive out of fear of discovery or because the Devil lives in our choice of a sensual nature and our mutual physical affection. We deceive casually, because it pleases us to, because we do no one harm, and because we enjoy accumulating venial sins.

We drive off under no clouds, although ahead on the path, far ahead, we can see a storm gathering to obscure our elders' sunlight. The road turns sharply at Deacon Hawley's second field, and we lose sight of our moral guidance. I urge the horse to take a left turn back toward the river, which plies to our favor. I find a spot, far from anyone's home because it is so close to the river's annual flooding. We alight and slide down the mud trail to the river. To our surprise, we undress completely, unafraid and truly as if we know what we are doing. But we know not what works we have in store. We know only the hushed mechanism of action, operating as if by a spring unwinding. We face one another, surprised by the clumsiness of our bodies. She takes me in her hand and turns herself around and lays hold of a tree trunk for support with her free hand. She guides me. It is not easy, contrary to what we expect of sin, but the pain, the sweat, the unaccustomed shapes conjured against the shadows in our minds, the very struggle, makes this action tangibly pleasing. Lilacs nearby color the surrounding smell.

Inside a small inlet of the river, we find a raft made of fallen logs with green willow branches as lashing. We climb onto it, now dimly aware our sin is great, but in the grip of a force that makes our movements, at least, seem sensible and clean-spirited. The boys who made the raft would not disfavor its being employed for a half hour. We intend only to drift in place in the tiny, protected bay, so we hang our clothes neatly on the bushes by the water. The raft does at first turn gently in soporific circles so at length we fall asleep in each other's arms. But rivers are mischievous spirits and, with a start, we wake to find ourselves midstream, downriver, past the ferry landing. We judge our chances of swimming ashore poor at this stage of the river, where it moves with cunning and authority. We do not yield to despair, however, and we see, from our lowly berth, the beauty of this river valley. The Connecticut River here comes to a great gap in the mountains, which are just this week a riot of new greens.

The raft moves quickly for a time, then it comes to a stretch of languid swirls, and water begins to penetrate the careless vessel. We luxuriate in the sensation of cold river water and hot sun above. Mortal danger also awakens carnal desire, so we move together again and hold each other as one scene gradually melts into the next. The notch in the Mount Holyoke Range comes closer. The stack of white clouds in the sky rests along this ridge, too, a pattern which is prophetic not of danger but of passage from one state of bliss to another. The opposite bank draws very near at this point. The raft drifts within easy reach of several roots and branches. The underbrush rustles, and two shiny foreheads flash. Two Indians lie on their stomachs, long sticks in their hands, confabulating about who knows what aspect of the inner workings of Nature. The Indians stand up, brown leaves painted on their flesh. We wave. The Indians stare unblinking at the white-skinned devils who are slowly sinking in each other's arms, unconcerned by the river that gathers us in its embrace. Even underwater, sunlight glints off our open eyes. We sit upright on the sandy bottom, breathing calmly as if we will survive the airless realm we have discovered. The Indians back away toward their canoe, more certain than ever that this once fertile meadow is hopelessly human.

JULY 1780
JOSEPH HAWLEY, 57

I sit in the mid-summer sun by the Connecticut River writing a letter to John Adams, who resides temporarily in Philadelphia guarding the tenets of this new Constitution I hold dear. I write the date, "July 26, 1780," but no more. Before the sun rises, my old mare leads me away from Pudding Lane. We ride out to this sand spit exposed in the dry months along the great river. Sleep is a rare pleasure. Of late, I see spirits at the foot of my bed. Not wishing to wake Mrs. Hawley, I walk the spirits out to the tomato garden and reason with them as well as I can. My own faculties are degrading, and these ghosts of Northampton's past are winning their arguments regularly. This early morn, a spirit alarmed me as much as any has: Mr. Edwards. When I was a young man, I participated in the expulsion of pastor Edwards. The correctness of this decision never lessened my regret that it happened (and my ambitions as a young barrister interfered with knowing accurately how correct I was). We reconciled several years after his expulsion, but Edwards died from an experimental small pox inoculation in the early days of his presidency of the College of New Jersey. He was always seeking ways to educate.

The vision of Jonathan Edwards at four o'clock this morning was of a man nearly defeated by the dread disease. His eyes were yellow and the sockets gray. His skin was sloughing off in long strips. He stooped, as if from the great pain in his bones, and I took the minister's pain personally. "Forgive me for having caused this calamity to you and your family, sir," I said. Edwards did not speak during the encounter, but the force of his logic drove me from my bed and then from my tomatoes. "My Dear Adams," I am able to write, at last. "I reprove my Self for not being at the Tavern when you return from your duties. The southern faction must make matters the more difficult by the day. I do not arrogate myself the role of Intermediary, as you yourself are, but I wish I could sit with you near that other great river, the Delaware. I hoped one day to participate in a small fashion. These letters provide some satisfaction. Listen to your old friend's madness. My obvious self-concern irritates my gout, but the continent's health is more important than my own. I've taken myself to this spot along the Connecticut. It does not clean the soul. The Self I valued so long betrays me."

A breeze kicks up, and willows a dozen paces away sweep the sand. A log floats by, not unlike a canoe an Indian might have navigated downstream. I pause in my writing, consider a swim. I want to soak the letter in my beloved River. But thoughts along the path of national ambitions take me back to Philadelphia.

Last night, we had Barry and Kay and Steve and Marsha over for dinner. Barry was recently hired in my own philosophy department, and Steve teaches in the government department. We are all liberal in outlook, with a surprising variance to these views. At one point, Marsha and Kay had a heated argument. Kay favors Bobby Kennedy, feeling he is the only logical outcome of the failing candidacy of Eugene McCarthy. Marsha is more pragmatic, and she supports Hubert Humphrey, despite his cowardice over Vietnam and his loyalty to his president, Lyndon Johnson. Kay was winning the argument. I was seated between Marsha and Kay. At the height of the argument, I thought a fistfight might break out between the two women, so I leaned over to Kay and said, loud enough for everyone to hear, "Let's go upstairs and make love." This stopped the shouting for just a moment. When talk resumed, we were all a little less noisy. No one responded to this suggestion of mine.

No one laughed, and no one objected. Jean gave me the briefest of glances, which may have indicated amusement. We are all disconcerted by the war, the violence in the cities, King's assassination, and the possibility that something good might actually come of this election. Martin Luther King was born four days before I was, in January 1929.

I told two stories during the evening. I don't recall how they were received, but they glow in my memory of the party.

When I had a cold as a child, I was bundled off to bed. Once my grandmother was visiting and joined me in the tent my mother constructed to capture the spewing fumes of eucalyptus and steam. Grandmother read to me from the Bible, and when she came to the part about the Pharaoh ordering the firstborn son of every family killed, I said, "That would be Gary, wouldn't it?" of my younger brother. "No, dear, that would be you," my grandmother said in her King James Bible voice.

It seems that Lenin's body became a liability for Stalin after the Second World War. He needed to transfer it out of the country for a while. Even dead and mummified, Lenin posed a threat, and Stalin couldn't do what he ordinarily did to enemies of the people—have them shot. Stalin called up Churchill in England. The soft socialist Attlee had no time for Stalin. But his old friend Churchill was working up his anti-communist bona fides. De Gaulle also was sympathetic, but unable to comply because he no longer had any power. Finally, in despair, Stalin got David Ben-Gurion on the line. "Sure," Ben-Gurion said. "No problem. But I should warn you, my country has the highest incidence of rising from the dead in the world."

Around midnight, Jean remembered the sponge cake and ice cream. I poured crème de menthe over each dessert. We continued talking, one on top of the other, until two. At some point, Barry stood up abruptly and said to Kay, "We should go." Steve and Marsha concurred. We all hugged in the front hall. The intensity of the disagreements seemed lost in the mists of alcohol and good talk. I noticed our middle child, Brian, on the front stairs about halfway up, wide-eyed and alert, leaning against a pillow. No one else seemed to see him. All four of our guests left without their coats. It was very cold outdoors, but Barry and Kay drove home, and Steve and Marsha had to walk only two doors down the street. Jean and I did dishes carelessly, laughing at this phrase or that joke from the evening. We stumbled to bed maybe half an hour later.

MAY 1738

TOM MATHEWS, 35

The shadow of a great oak gathered a small crowd outside the meeting house on Main Street. We could hear a thundering sermon inside, but not the words themselves. Now the holy voice stilled, and all we heard was the creaking of the benches, coughs, one embarrassed sneeze cut short. Oftentimes we, who were not among the elect, would try to listen to the sermon, but we would end quietly chatting among ourselves, aware that we should keep peaceful and avoid spontaneous outburst. This day was unusual. At the center of the excitement was myself, the humble ferry master. I was not ordinarily paid much respect. I was known to drink spirits to excess and had once been questioned for embracing my wife on the doorstep. I also had a tendency to tell stories with too much zeal and joy, despite warnings to keep to the point and not overelaborate. Such a reputation usually sequestered me. This Sunday I blushed at the attention all eyes paid me, and, for once, I was shy of telling the story again of this star-crossed couple, children of the River Gods, who had not been seen since the ferry master bade them well on the Hadley side of the river, four days past.

I inhaled the smell of leather and sweat and exhaled all evil thoughts. I said, "They evinced a holy pleasure at the soft air. The boy read scriptures as they departed. The girl stumbled once and let out a cry but not a licentious sound, only a fearful noise, perhaps at a spider on her breath. The buckboard stood near the banks of Hadley Meadows, no trace of them here-abouts." These lies frightened me. I had bundled the clothes I found and tied a rock to them and thrown the packet far into the river current. I knew what to make of the arrangement— or disarrangement—of the clothes. This surprised me by not pleasing me in any way. She was a beautiful girl and the boy a much stronger force of nature than I ever was. But when the two reverends returned, stern in their anxiety, I did not tell them of my discovery. Was this wrong? Was I already under the sway of evil, somehow colluding with the sin I had just missed witnessing?

The next night, certain townspeople convinced me to meet them by the Mill River, at the first ford. One brought a bottle of cider he had no difficulty encouraging me to believe was medicinal. It did indeed taste like health. Many were not convinced of my earlier story. Shaking, I recanted. After much prodding, I told another tale.

"I had often before this said that if the Indians should come, I would choose rather to be killed by them than taken alive, but when it came to the trial my mind changed. Their glittering weapons so daunted my spirit that I chose to go along with those (I may say) ravenous beasts, than to end my days at that moment. They were some twenty in number, all naked and surrounding the girl often in a frenzy, if you'll excuse my describing it so. The boy they killed quickly, a wooden bat to the temple of his head, for crying out too often. In the heavy brush north of Hatfield, I eluded my shadow. My surprise that they did not return for me was lessened by the great spider-webbed forest I fell into, dozens of the creatures crisscrossing the branches, most the size of my closed fist. I paid very careful attention to these beings because, though I feared them greatly, they seemed to protect me from the wrath of these silent, stealthy men. What came of the girl? I dread to say they had loosened off all her garments and she seemed to find joy in the naked gait, running as quickly and quietly as these wild animals, not as if she were a prisoner. They must have cast a spell on her."

The townsmen were more satisfied with this story, even if I was not—Pastor Edwards could demolish it with one word. I drank quickly, both of the cider and later of whisky. No one was surprised that I died three weeks later after an outbreak of smallpox. The bodies of the two cousins were never found. The Indian villages to the north and west were eventually razed, but not because of these abductions.

I stand before the congregation today to tell you why I do not want to be confirmed into Edwards Church. I am sorry if my words make you feel uncomfortable, but I have been asked to speak honestly. I would like to talk of Jonathan Edwards, the man this church was named after. We have moved a long way from the days of his congregation in the 1700s, before he was fired for either encouraging children to report on their parents' sins or for spending too much money on his own children— there is much debate about this. Many of the things Edwards worried about are not fashionable or even much talked about today. But the Hell that Jonathan Edwards describes intrigues me. Let me read from a famous sermon:

> Imagine yourself to be cast into a fiery oven, all of a glowing heat, or into the midst of a glowing brick-kiln, or of a great furnace, where your pain would be

as much greater than that occasioned by accidentally touching a coal of fire. Imagine also that your body were to lie there for a quarter of an hour, full of fire, all the while full of quick sense. How long would that quarter of an hour seem to you.

Mr. Edwards asks his congregation to imagine the pain of liquid fire for a day, a month, a year, and then all of eternity. This is not his only argument for being good. He also portrays an indifferent God, unwilling or unable to intervene on our behalf. But the description of the pain of Hell is a large part of this warning and one of the reasons the sermon was so effective. I am familiar with pain myself. Since I was a boy I have had what our own Doctor Rogers calls migraine headaches. Five minutes of one of these headaches can be as bad as five hours. I imagine that five days of a migraine would be unbelievably painful. And yet I wonder if I might not become accustomed to the pain at some point. Is it not possible that I would, after a time, begin to enjoy the pain? This sounds odd, but this is the problem I have with the Hell devised by Jonathan Edwards. You may say that it is a small fight to pick with this sect of Christianity. Hell is not such a large part of the sermons I've listened to, since I've been invited upstairs for the adult services. Maybe Mr. Beebee has talked about Hell at other times, when I wasn't here. But it seems to me a flaw in any Hell you can imagine—fire and brimstone, nails in the skin, torture for infinity, unimaginable pain. If you know you can't die from the pain, perhaps the pain will lose its ability to frighten you. Pain without the threat of death cannot have the same effect as pain that might cause you to die. The only real torture I can anticipate would be from boredom, but one would be as prone to that in Heaven as in Hell. That's another kind of heresy, though.

Edwards used to pray five times a day in secret and spend many hours in religious talk with other boys. He used to meet with these boys for group prayer. He said he experienced indescribable delight in religion. He and some of his schoolmates built a booth in the swamp, in a very secret place, for prayer. I feel nothing remotely like this ecstasy. I am nothing like this young man was. This is not a useful comparison, but the distance between Jonathan Edwards and my own spiritual makeup is too great to believe I am anything like a formally religious person.

The idea of making me stand in front of you to explain why I don't want to be confirmed is dishonest intimidation. If you are confirmed, you don't have to say anything. If you refuse to be confirmed, you have to stand in front of 200 people and speak embarrassing truths. It should be just as difficult to join this church as it is to reject it. It is ironic that just before Jonathan Edwards was fired by the town, a man asked to join the church and he was ready to admit his faith—he was a believer. But the rules of the church did not require him to confess his faith, so he said he did not want to. Edwards was fired because he said he could divine who had faith and who did not. Now, only those children like me, who have no faith, need describe it. Those who claim to have faith in Christ and the church sit mute behind me. I am sorry. I choose not to join this faith.

Joseph Hawley, 27: Jonathan Edwards would be the judge of our hearts. My father slit his throat in 1731 during the Great Awakening that Edwards had a large role in fomenting. I do not blame Parson Edwards for my father's death. Father loved his melancholy more than he loved his family or his faith. I am a young man, just embarked on a marriage my mother opposed (so she lives at the other end of our house on Pudding Lane, rarely deigning to address my wife). I have no children to worry over yet. But I do worry about the methods the parson employs for judging who will not become members of the church.

Jonathan Edwards, 46: Since I settled in the work of the ministry, in this place, I have had a peculiar concern for the souls of the young people and a desire that religion might flourish among them. This is what I have longed for, and vice, vanity, and disorder among our youth has been grievous to me. It was from this grief that I led this church to measures for suppressing vice among our young people, which gave so great offence and by which I became so obnoxious to the town. I have sought the good and not the harm of our young people. I have desired their happiness. If it was plain to all that I was under the infallible guidance of Christ, then I should have power over my flock. I should have power to teach them what they ought to do.

Seth Pomeroy, 44: He locks himself away and reads. He reads too much. His sermons printed on fine paper are well and good, if one has the patience for such stuff. He is an intoxicated visionary who presumes to see the will of God. We might be better served by a more vigorous and open-air man, a friend of the farms and the river and the cattle. How will Parson Edwards know the truth of a man's heart and sinfulness if he knows only what he reads? A man's vigor might be mistaken for sin. One of our elders said the more learned and witty you are, the more likely Satan will employ you. I make guns. I am a soldier. I know what I know because I can feel it in my hands.

Jonathan Edwards, 46: I take the greatest delight in the Bible. I feel a harmony between something in my heart and those sweet and powerful words. I see so much light, exhibited by every sentence. Such a refreshing, ravishing food is communicated. I sometimes dwell on one sentence to see the wonders contained in it, and yet every sentence of the scriptures seems to be full of wonders. I am even glad to read such corrupt books as *A Treatise on Human Nature*, by David Hume, a man of considerable, though wayward, genius. I read what I must to learn the tools of hewing, planing, and squaring away a child's sins. I must not argue with churchgoers when I cannot handsomely retreat from the argument. My travels and fame interfere with the proper mission of my ministry. The town trusted my grandfather Solomon Stoddard implicitly. The days of a minister's complete dominion over a town are perhaps gone and done. The young merchants and lawyers wish to govern the town as if it were an organization of bodies, not souls. Family government has decayed, and fathers no longer keep sons from prowling at night. Neighbors are full of contention, and, instead of being knit close together as one man in mutual love, they bring lawsuits, and lawyers thrive. Militia days become orgies, and women wear false locks and display naked breasts in the way of befuddled men on the turnpike. Townspeople betray a marked disposition to tell lies, especially when selling anything. The business morality of even the most righteous leaves much to be desired: the wealthy speculate in land, and day laborers and mechanics are unreasonable in their demands. Too many men are emissaries of atheism, lechery, paganism, and democracy. One pulls against the reins of this speeding four-in-hand carriage to no avail. I prefer to write.

Joseph Hawley, 27: The scores of discouraging conversations at town meetings about Jonathan Edwards' rules for membership in the church had one unintended benefit. Democracy is an old idea, but, as Milton says, it can shake a powerful arsenal. Parson Edwards wanted the rule of a single aristocrat, himself. He wanted to judge who could join the church himself, although this idea came to him slowly. I am a young man and a lawyer. I confess to my own grave sin of pride and hubris in this matter. But when Colonel John Stoddard died three years ago, so died the last link to Colonel Stoddard's father, the Reverend Solomon Stoddard. Colonel Stoddard was a great man and a great ruler. Without him, the town turned to its own devices for governance. Without him, Parson Edwards lost an important ally, and I don't think he realized how important this alliance was. I see novel forms of government in the offing here. I am excited by this change, just as I am distressed by my mentor's stubbornness and fall. Pastor Edwards trained me for my education, and I was close to becoming a minister myself, before the law seduced me. I know this decision will haunt me, but I feel great things on the horizon, for the town and perhaps for the nation.

The deaf are nimble and sudden. Our faces are alert and simple, like the face of a raccoon caught in a flashlight beam. We lack a subtle wavering aura of response to sound. I'm a resident adviser to a floor of other deaf students here at the Clarke School in Northampton in western Massachusetts. Unlike all my charges, I once heard birds sing and my mother coo sweet nothings in my ear in Princeton, Illinois. I was always deaf in one ear, then an infection took the hearing in the other ear when I was six. This isolates me from the girls in my dorm. I don't mind. I walk alone late at night around this town, which, interestingly, sent the first settlers to my farm town in Illinois in the 1800s. Our dorm was formerly the Prospect Hotel, a famous spa when Round Hill drew tired New Yorkers and Bostonians for its healing waters. I walk a lot at night because I can't sleep. In the last month, phantom sounds penetrate my consciousness just as I'm about to drift off. I'm a senior, so I schedule my classes in the afternoon and sleep all morning—the sun seems to aid me. I "hear" stray noises and conversations. I am reading all the Henry James I can get my hands on lately. He stayed at the Prospect Hotel in his early twenties, so that may explain why I think I'm overhearing his conversations and other talk about him. I have gotten used to the voices. The odd sound still startles me—a toilet flushing, floorboards creaking, a woman's voice moaning in the room next to mine. Harry, as James called himself then, talks to the woman through his adjacent wall, earnestly reassuring her. But she must be asleep. She never answers.

OCTOBER 1731
JONATHAN EDWARDS, 28
A SOUL DEPARTING

I rise between four and five each morning, and I spend thirteen hours a day in study. My usual diversion is riding on horseback, and I decide before leaving home what should be the subject of my thought. I pin a piece of paper to my coat and charge my mind to associate what I have written on the paper. I repeat the process with a second paper and a second train of thought, sometimes returning from my ride with many such papers. After the ride, I take the papers from my coat in regular order, and I write down the line of thought and the conclusion that each has suggested. Absorbed in meditation, I am usually not mindful of anything around me. This day, with many papers attached to my summer coat pertaining to a recent unorganized awakening in the Valley, I come upon a naked white woman on the trail to Hatfield, adjacent to the Connecticut River. I do not recognize her from any of the nearby congregations. She has one hand buried in the orifice out of which children are birthed. She screams violently, especially when I touch ground near her. I see from her bright red belly that she is in some kind of devilish labor, the end of which will be death, not a child. I pull her hand out, bloody. I hold this red hand against my white shirt and for a moment her screams abate. A beatific look loosens her facial muscles. She speaks a word, "Clean," which I have to agree with. Then her stomach clenches, and with a terrible burp a purple monstrosity falls from her belly. It seems, for a moment, alive. I discern eyes—more than two, many fingers more than ten, a sort of head, but no neck, no legs, no nose. I firmly hold the girl's hand, although I feel my own legs and bowels twitch in an awful way. I soil myself, and a sob rises out of me. The girl says, "Touch me, God Almighty, touch me." I know not how to interpret these words, but my other hand reaches involuntarily for her belly, still ruby red but slack now, and I rub it. She sighs so loudly that nearby leaves move as if from a breeze. This is her soul departing. Her head falls backwards, and black bile spills out of her sweet mouth. I use my knife to dig the earth and bury the child. I stand up with the girl in my arms, lay her across my horse's saddle, and walk with them back to town. I pull the papers from my coat and put them in my pocket. I do not want to remember what I set my mind to consider this day. Another set of images has impressed itself on my soul.

My grandfather stands up in a meadow near the LaFleur Airport, and for an instant the Piper Cub taking off behind him gives him wings. Then the small plane and my grandfather separate, and Eric peers into his handmade butterfly net, eyes cataloging the contents of the fine white linen, a fog of insects he did not desire flying out around his head. The plane swooshes over both my grandfather and my older brother, who just perceptibly duck their heads at the noise. My brother and I love nothing in the world more than our grandfather. Eric winks at Geoffrey and disappears into the shoulder-high cattails. I sit on a log, bored, refusing to join in the bug collecting, but also refusing to let Geoffrey have Eric all to himself. Geoff is fifteen years old, too young to have the thoughts he has, he is told by adults. Eric is one of the few adults who listens to us as equals. For instance, when Geoff said, a little while ago, that it seems his worst fears about the Nixon administration are coming true six months into his presidency, our grandfather does not make a joke or say he's Canadian. Eric says Nixon reminds him of a boss he once had, bright and hard-working and full of good ideas, but unaccountably insecure and consumed by slights and paranoia and the thought that a number of colleagues were out to take his job, which in fact they were and did. Geoff says he's worried Nixon is going to cause nuclear war. Eric says very seriously that we all ought to be prepared to meet our maker, but we should fight this nuclear madness with every ounce of our strength. Then he says, "But if the world is about to end, let's make sure we stop by the McDonald's on King Street and pick up some fries and milk shakes."

The ringing startles me out of sleep—the persistent ringing—and then a woman's voice (from beyond the grave). I lift the coffin and listen, the smooth black receiver cradled in my trembling hand. "Mr. President, Mr. President," I hear eventually. My rocking chair stops rocking. I glance up Massasoit Street toward Elm Street, and out of the corner of my eye I note the gardener trembling. He has a fine persistent tremble, chin, hands, shoulders, but it does not interfere with his lovely work. "You were having a bad dream, sir?" he says. I nod, neck still tingling, my whole left side tingling and numb, for that matter. Mother's voice rings in my mind, but also her smell—neither present to my senses for fifty years—like a box of used souls. I see a young man edging his way down the street. Many drive or walk by the house since we returned from Washington. Mrs. Coolidge urges me to sell the duplex and move somewhere more private and fitting for an ex-president.

I demur. The young man's face is vaguely familiar. He finds the courage to walk past my porch. He stops. He speaks. "I was a boy, standing at the fence outside the White House, Mr. President. Your friend, a colonel, saw me and brought me in to meet you. I could not find the voice to talk, but the colonel spoke for me, telling you how sorry I was that you'd lost your son. It moved me to see the president cry." Calvin Coolidge, Jr. developed a blister after playing tennis on the White House courts. The blister became infected and he died of septicemia in Walter Reed General Hospital, July 7, 1924. The country may have listened on the radio, but it did not hear the boy say, "I surrender." Mrs. Coolidge will die many years after I do, but I note that she'll do so just a few hours after the thirty-second anniversary of Calvin Coolidge, Jr.'s death.

JULY 1972
BRIAN KITELEY, 15

An angel smoking a cigarette sits down next to me on the steps
of an old bank in Springfield, Massachusetts, five in the morning, late July. I took the train from Montreal, after visiting my
grandparents. The train passed through my hometown at about
three in the morning but did not stop there. I got off the train
at Springfield, half an hour later. The bus station was closed,
so I camped on the worn granite steps of this former bank,
now a mortuary. My cigarette-smoking angel is somewhere
between twenty and thirty. She is shaking and her skin looks
like wax paper. She asks where I'm going. I say Northampton.
"To the rehab clinic at the State Hospital? I have *got* to get up
there again," she says. "They don't make you feel stupid, just
fucked up."

It is going to be a hot day, and already it is comfortably warm,
but this woman, who is theoretically beautiful, snuggles against

my shoulder, her teeth chattering. I ask her name. "Daisy," she says. She does not want to know my name. A big boxy car drives slowly past us, windows tinted black. Daisy shouts, "I'm not going back." The car stops. Smoke curls out of the driver's window, which is on the other side from us. We are high enough to see the reflection of the driver in the big plate glass of the bus station cafeteria across the street, but I am afraid to look in his direction. Daisy makes a pushing motion with her left hand, as if urging a horse on, and the car does go, more slowly still. When it rounds the corner, up the street toward the train station, I let out a breath. "You got no reason to worry, honey," Daisy says. "You're going to Northampton." After a moment, she says, "You're not going to the State Hospital. You *live* in Northampton, don't you? You walk to school down one of those tree-lined streets near the college campus. Your parents put a jungle gym and a swimming pool in the backyard." She is right, except for the pool and the jungle gym. I tell her how strange it was to take the train through Northampton and not be able to get off. I say it felt like I was a ghost, going through Hatfield and then along King Street until we passed over Bridge Street—for a second we could see downtown Northampton, completely dark, not a soul in the center of town.

Daisy asks me how old I am. Instead of answering, I ask how old she is. "You're a shrink in training wheels, I see. I'm seventeen," she says. "Been on the road for three years. Celebrated my birthday in Syracuse." I say, "Seventeen," all by itself an admission of my own inexperience and youth—I am fifteen. She leans away from me, as if she were about to light a cigarette out of the wind, and she vomits. She says, "Sorry. You got a handkerchief?" I have a cloth one my grandmother gave me at the train station, which I hand to Daisy. She stands and cleans herself. I glance at the neat pool of vomit, which is blue and green, with tiny threads of blood. We shift down a few steps, but she sits with a foot between us. "I don't suppose you want to take me to Northampton, now?" she says. I imagine calling my parents, seeing my father's sympathetic worried eyes in the rearview mirror an hour later, and I don't answer for a moment. She says, "No need to get off your fucking ass." She takes hold of the back of my neck in a way no one ever has, and she kisses me softly on the lips, leaving behind the slightest taste of fermented pizza. She jumps up and her incredibly silky hair slips through my pathetic fingers. She walks quickly around the corner. I have to wait for the painful erection to subside before I can stand up. On the next street, I see her opening the door of the big car. An arm reaches out and jerks her in.

Calvin Coolidge's law practice was mainly trusts and estates when he was a young lawyer in Northampton. As president of the United States, to my astonishment, Coolidge has not completely given up this practice. I am a lawyer at Coolidge & Hemenway, and one of my jobs the past half year is to take the train monthly to Washington. I am ushered into the Oval Office to present President Coolidge with drafts of probate court filings for review and signature. He tells me he just can't give up the fees. I am often led through a typical president's day, when Coolidge feels events are not too sensitive or pressing. Coolidge says the two occupations—small-town lawyer and president of the United States—do not demand such different skills. "With each, you sign papers, you ask questions of trusted advisors, read their faces more than their answers, and you go out into the town or city and smile as much as your face will allow. The president shouldn't do too much—he shouldn't *know* too much."

My bosses tell me Coolidge doesn't say a lot, and that is the story being passed on by the national press, as much out of ridicule as out of admiration. This is not true in private, when he is signing papers and doing the quick legal work aloud. He is chatty and seems to have a great deal of time to spend with me. Once I ask if the story is true that a woman sitting next to him at a dinner made a bet that she could make him say more than two words. Coolidge's reply was, "You lose." The president nods at this anecdote. "She was a handsome woman," he says. "When I said, 'you lose,' those weren't the only words I said to the woman that night. They were a joke on my reputation. Mrs. Coolidge was in Vermont visiting relatives. I sat with this woman for several hours. If the president does not get up from the dinner table no one else does, and eventually I saw the discomfort in the room. I do not mean to say that I was flirting with this woman, other than that one remark. But I missed Grace, and the company of this witty woman was a temporary replacement for my wife. At one point I slipped and told this woman we were urging our proxies in the courts to impede the organization of labor unions, a small confession of an administration secret." He pauses. "I don't know why I told her that detail. Grace's absence was enough to make me talkative, and that is not a good thing for a president." The president is silent now. I sweep up the signed documents. I place them carefully in my briefcase. We part company warmly. He asks his partner Hemenway to bring the probate court material himself next month.

I am supporting George McGovern for President, and I send money that my husband Richard gives me, but I use it furtively and give much less than I would otherwise. I am not capable of earning anything like it. So I sign my maiden name to a McGovern ad, and Richard is happy not to have his name splashed across the local newspaper. It makes him feel superior to think I support somebody who can't win. He will vote for the man when it comes down to it, which makes me crazy.

A sweet melancholy boy from two blocks away rings the doorbell, "canvassing" for McGovern. Geoffrey Kiteley admits up front he won't be old enough to vote this fall, but he is passionate about the man, articulate, heartbreakingly unaware of how little chance he has. Still, this young man listens to my questions, ponders them for a long while, and answers very slowly and intelligently. This has been his manner since he was eight years old, and it has nothing to do with feminism, but I like to think it's been planted well.

When my art dealer from Newbury Street in Boston arrived the other day—a much anticipated and nerve-wracking business—Richard firmly kept the conversation out of my hands, doing all the talking, dismissing everything I had to say, as though Pete were president of the AMA, and John had to toady and impress. Several men from the neighborhood visited after that, and John told one he'd spent the last few days walking all Lisa's men to the door. As if to say, "Am I not the modern man, and ain't she some sex object!" Nobody could possibly be interested in what I have to say. I think I am righteously angry because I agreed to be an amusing hobby all my married life. Meanwhile Richard usually approaches my painting with the idea that he could do it better. This burst of anger lets a proper amount of adrenaline loose and I may use it to good purpose in the "studio," i.e., the kitchen.

I learned yesterday that one of my neighbors is in the habit of giving her husband (who is a very good friend of ours) his lunch sandwich on a piece of paper towel. Seems so impersonal, so "You can take this sandwich or leave it." I don't know what to make of that gesture. I'm for it and I'm against it. This women's consciousness-raising business will have to mark mine "condemned."

Richard and I go to the Majestic in Easthampton—filthy seats, a smattering of filthy guilty-looking men in the audience, and a movie called "The Filthy Five." Dear man that he is, Richard is visibly embarrassed when we walk into the theater late to see on screen a huge close-up of a penis ejaculating—he chooses that moment to take his glasses off and clean them, breathing on the lenses in nice rhythm to the motion on-screen. I am intrigued to see what does arouse Richard, despite his trying to hide it—a woman's long-fingernailed hand holding this astoundingly large cock—not her breasts from behind (which I find surprisingly seductive), nor the curves of her belly or thighs. We live on the front end of a messy tidal wave, intermingled with all the seaweed and ocean trash and driftwood.

Douglas, Nathan, Jon, and I go down to the Mill River on Friday nights. Three of us are seniors in high school; Nathan is a junior. We always bring marijuana along to smoke, which the others enjoy more than I do now. I was the first to suggest it and I'm still the one to buy the lid from Swanson in the Child's Park forest off the rose garden, but in plain view of his father's office—Swanson's father is the high school principal. The trouble is, marijuana increases my gloom. I used to consider this black mood a result of the world around us—our failing governments, the war in Vietnam, the coming Ice Age, the cowardly abdication of Johnson, the re-election of Nixon—until I realized it was just me. I like men's bodies and their private parts. So I feel a kind of generalized despair, though all the other root effects—war, climate, politics, American capitalism grinding down its underclass—still hold. Douglas read somewhere recently about the Northampton Association, a group of proto-hippies in the 1840s who started a commune to produce silk in Florence, where he lives. Douglas is Douglas Adam, and he says he's descended from the William Adam of the association—with absolutely no proof of this fact. His mother brought him to Northampton after her divorce in Lancaster, Ohio. This utopian community has colored our discussion for the past few Fridays. I grow tired of the enthusiasm. We've already lost one of our group of friends to a Christian cult in Texas, God knows how. Douglas wears silk scarves and three-piece suits to school when everyone else wears jeans and army jackets. To shut Douglas up, I propose a walk, after our first joint. We both prefer to leaven the high with exercise, while Jon and Nathan prefer to vegetate, staring at the river and the moonlight and the occasional fish jumping. It's a good arrangement, because Nathan and Jon are straight. Douglas and I walk off about a half mile for quick, perfunctory blow jobs. This is my first sex, if you don't count the girl a year and a half ago.

It surprises me to feel no love for Douglas. I like him a great deal, and I assume Douglas likes me. But we agree, without saying so, that this is mainly for the sake of practice. I do catch myself picturing Douglas's pants coming all the way down, and him turning his luscious backside toward me, but… Who I love is Nathan. I don't pretend Nathan will ever reciprocate. This too is useful, though. It forces a kind of noble renunciation on me. The one man I find deliciously attractive I know I'll never have, not because Nathan doesn't see me the same way, but because he doesn't see me, period. Nathan looks right through me. He admires my mind. He seems to be looking at that—or maybe he's just stoned all the time.

Afterwards, Douglas and I return to the little compound we've fashioned at a bend in the river, behind a small forest. We've trampled down river grass and dragged some logs to the clearing. To get to this spot, we have to walk through water a couple of dozen yards, but it's usually shallow and sometimes almost dry. Douglas and I come upon Nathan and Jon, in absolute silence. The two friends probably have not said a word for minutes. Jon picks up the conversation he and Douglas had started half an hour before. He says, "So, if we agree that the members of the Northampton Association were radicals, meaning, abolitionists, perfectionists, and temperance supporters, then it was a form we can't conceive of now. The association was both Christian and hard left, as interested in human perfectibility as they were in communal—read, communist—values. They believed in both things."

Nathan says, "Would you shut up, Jon. You're ruining what had been up to this point a perfectly serviceable high."

DECEMBER 1894
SETH COOKE, 50

Terry Cooke, yeoman from Kent, Old England, staked out his share of land and built his hut in Northampton, in 1698. He had married his second cousin Rose, and in due time a family of ten children gathered about them. The Cookes expanded their households, died, were born, died, emigrated west, and finally, after nearly two centuries, there were none left, except me, a fifty-year-old bachelor. My hut was a few dozen paces from the Mill River, between Northampton and Florence. It was much like my ancestor's first hut, whose land now gave way to the new college. I was Seth Cooke. I collected potatoes or nuts when they were ready, shooting at rabbits but mostly missing them, trapping the occasional squirrel for a bit of meat.

On a regular basis, I met a young woman in the clearing beside my hut. She said she came from one of the colleges nearby.

She asked questions, because she was curious about the history I had in my head. She brought a notebook, and she wrote down what I said, which bothered me, but I could not read, so I made sour jokes at her expense, which she also wrote down. I fed her what I was able to. She never brought her own victuals, not even drink. I made beer, and I never offered any. It seemed improper. The walk from her home was about an hour, and I regretted being unable to give her well water, which was tainted. Beer was my only liquid. I told her stories, but soon these bored me, so I made up stories, which she did not notice were untrue. The college teacher originally came from a town near Boston, and she had an accent and a husky voice that disturbed me, but I held my peace.

One day, as the leaves were turning brown, and the air was cold around the edges, I could no longer stand it and offered her a beer. To my alarm she accepted. I had offered only to be able to drink beer myself. She praised the taste, as if she knew what she was talking about. I stood to my full height, which was a few inches below her full height—she stood too. I put my wooden mug down and she imitated this behavior. I ordered her to enter the hut. She laughed at the tone of my voice, but she obeyed.

Once inside, I pulled at her skirt, which came off in one long piece of wool. Her undergarments were voluminous, so she was hardly undressed, but she cried out and fainted dead away. I worked at all the rest of her many layers, cursing the complex fasteners, buttons, and zippers. Eventually she was unclothed. I did not know what to do, nor what to think. She had no breasts. I recalled dimly my sister's body, but she died at thirteen, and I could not see any memory of my mother who died the following year. It was decided to rub this woman with oils, which I had in abundance: walnut, hemp, thistle, and sunflower oils that I sold and bartered in Florence. Her skin was rough and tanned and hairy and full of lesions, as if she had weighed a great deal more than she did now. I had the same lesions because of my year of the runs when I lost a good deal of weight. Between her legs was something that looked like what was between my legs. I had imagined that women were different down there.

The action of massaging these oils into her slowly brought her back to thoughtfulness. She took note of her state, but she did not scream again. She asked what was going on. A voice told her. She asked why. The voice said, "I do not know." It seemed the only thing to do. She began to ask her historical questions again. The thought of her notebook caused me to ask if she needed it. She said yes. I brought her the surprisingly heavy book and her quill pen and her inkwell. She sat up in the bed, and my hands continued to knead the lotions into her skin, pulling her legs apart and paying particular attention to the very soft skin between these limbs. My hands came close to where the legs came together. Her small thing began to grow larger and larger. She asked questions. I did not answer. I was tired of the game. She wrote something down anyway. I asked her what answers she was writing. She read an answer, and it was a great deal like what I used to tell her. We continued this way for a long while. Finally, she asked me if I was going to have my way with her. I did not know what that meant. She told me to take my pants off. My hands wrestled with the buttons, and the fabric fell to the ground. My thing flopped out. She reached over and touched it. I think I shouted. She did not back away, and she did not laugh or cry. I had never touched myself down there. On her deathbed, my mother made me promise I never would. The history teacher told me in very plain words what I should do with my thing. She took hold of it until it was larger. It made several spasms and released a liquid. She said it didn't matter. She would not let go of the thing and after a moment it grew big again. She lay down on her stomach. She instructed me move on top of her. She pulled and I pushed. It was difficult to enter her hole.

The history teacher asked me to do this thing and that. She was very bold. When we were done, it was sad. I had to hold my hands around her neck for a long time. She was surprisingly strong. I buried her in the forest down the hill. I did this with great care, lifting her in a way that did not soil her any more than I already had done. I burned her clothes and pen, and I emptied her ink into the soil. I noted the spot for several weeks afterward. I used the ink bottle for oil. I could not make myself burn her book. I lay in bed in the late afternoon, pretending to read it, until one day I felt I had discerned some elements of the truth buried in it, buried with her. The lies I had told her turned out to be more truthful and accurate than the true stories. The lies made me tie around my neck a rope, which I also looped over an extended branch of the oak tree above her grave, after the first snow of December.

I died but continued for some time to see down into her grave. Her body held mysteries not even death cleared up. When my corpse was found, no one dug up her grave by the oak tree. They buried my body at Bridge Street Cemetery.

Keefe's lips are planted on a window of the second-story glass bridge that joins the two science buildings on the Smith College campus. Keefe is speaking softly to a woman walking directly below him, quiet words she cannot possibly hear, whose softness belie their violent sexual content. He is suggesting things I have not yet even imagined. I am several years away from experiencing half of what Keefe now mentions. Briefly, accidentally, she looks up at Keefe, and he steps back as if he'd been slapped. "Whoa!" he says. "She wants me, Kiteley." Indeed, a faint sneer passes across her lips, which I think can be interpreted as yearning, if you are as obsessed with sex as Keefe is.

I've never learned Keefe's first name. We all go by last names. Keefe and I have worked together for three weeks this summer in the sub-basement of McConnell Hall, employed by the college to do menial labor. We wash rat and rabbit shit out of cage trays in the biology lab. Today, we've been called into the office of Professor Walser, a fortyish German woman who is our temporary boss. We expect to be reprimanded for playing football with a plastic skull we found in the storage area—we thought it was plastic, until Keefe dropped a pass and the skull smashed in a very bone-like fashion. Miss Walser has a television on in her cluttered office showing men at long tables looking uncomfortable in front of the camera—the Watergate hearings. "This is important educational material. I will give you the rest of the afternoon off, for your promise to watch it." Keefe is overjoyed, but I am worried. Our actual boss is a round man named Nowicki, a supervisor in Buildings and Grounds. Miss Walser has pulled us away from the more ordinary dorm cleaning details he sees to. Nowicki distrusts her because she is a professor, a woman, and a European, so he appears from time to time for pop inspections, to make sure his boys are working. Miss Walser objects to these sudden appearances, but she cannot prevent them. I have the idea of holding a broom and Keefe finds a window squeegee in case Nowicki comes by. Keefe relaxes happily in Miss Walser's comfortable rolling chair, completely unconcerned, and he switches channels. I object. I don't want to disappoint Miss Walser, and I am actually interested in the hearings.

"Pussy," Keefe says, when I switch stations back to the hearings, but he says this gently, almost affectionately. I am a fascinating specimen to Keefe. Unlike the other guys my age who work for B&G, I have admitted I have not had sex. This gives Keefe unlimited ammunition against me, if he chooses to use it, but in the end he finds my status touching. It allows him to act as adviser, older brother, or pimp, depending on his moods. "She's not bad-looking for forty-four," Keefe says. I feel myself redden. I ask Keefe how he knows Miss Walser's age. "You can tell by her pussy hairs, the outer rim curling to gray." I laugh, but Keefe takes hold of my wrist and squeezes hard. "Don't think I couldn't, if I set my mind to it. But there's an easier way to determine pussy hair color. You look at the last bit of hair on the back of her neck. It comes from the same thoughts pussy hair comes from." I ask him not to use that word so often. "You prefer cunt or vagina, Professor Kiteley?" I hear footsteps in the hall and sit upright with my broom at the ready, a ridiculous pose. Nowicki stops at the doorway. He says nothing for a long while. Keefe leans back in his chair, creaking it, the squeegee in one hand, and he licks the rubber edge in one long motion. "Mmm," he says. "Tastes like pussy." Nowicki bursts out laughing. He falls against the doorway, holding his big belly. "You kill me, Keefe. You really could kill me." His laughter dies down. He says, "Now get to work, you pussies." Other footsteps resound in the hall, and Nowicki tries to stand straight, which is very difficult for him. He prefers giving orders from the chair in his "office," a basement room under a dormitory where we punch our time cards. Miss Walser arrives and squeezes past Nowicki, who is too dumbfounded to move out of her way. "I thought the boys should watch this historical event, Mr. Nowicki," Miss Walser says. "Oh, I, uh," he says. "It's only this one afternoon," Miss Walser says. "They have worked quite hard today. Surely it's important to see democracy in action. Don't you think?" Nowicki loses control of his face, which forms a fierce grin as if she's offered him a food whose name he cannot pronounce. "Just this once I guess it's okay," he says, and he leaves. Keefe lets out a wild laugh. Miss Walser looks so hard at him, that for once he falls silent. "Sorry, m'am," I say.

The three of us watch John Dean and his wife squirm for the rest of the afternoon, and I regret not being alone with Keefe to hear his graphic commentary on the bizarrely comic yet beautiful Mrs. Dean. At one point, John Dean says, "The conversation then turned to the use of the Internal Revenue Service to attack our enemies. I recall telling the president that we had not made much use of this because the White House didn't have the clout to get it done, that the IRS was a rather Democratically oriented bureaucracy and it would be very dangerous to try any such activities. The president seemed somewhat annoyed and said that the Democratic Administration had used this tool well and after the election we would get people in these agencies who would be responsive to the White House requirements." Keefe lets out a long low whistle, and he turns the sound down on the set. He says, "They're fucked now. This really fucks Nixon."

Miss Walser does not seem to react to the word *fuck*, but she disagrees with Keefe in a surprisingly vehement tone. I expect her to be anti-Nixon, the way the vast majority of my father's colleagues are. Keefe says, "All the rest of this crap is no smoking gun, but when you bring in the IRS, you're playing with fire. The unions won't stand for that. I know unions." Miss Walser says the antiwar activists are funded by the Democrats, and no matter what Nixon did he was justified in battling these extralegal forces at work to undermine the American democratic way of life. "Bullshit," Keefe says. He stands up and faces Miss Walser, who is sitting on the ledge of her high lab table. Their faces come within inches of each other. He smiles weirdly, as if he were feeling a piece of beef in his teeth, and Miss Walser does not back off one bit. I have to look away. When I turn back, Keefe is at the television, turning up the sound.

We watch in silence for the rest of the afternoon. We leave her office at three to punch our time cards, but Keefe surprises me yet again and says he wants to go back to Miss Walser's office to watch the remainder of the hearings. I ask him if he wants to be alone with her. Keefe gives me the same odd smile he gave her, but he does not answer. We return to her office, and she has strong black coffee waiting for us.

In July, Mary Bartlett, wife of Samuel Bartlett, sickened and died. The best minds of the town could not make a narrative of her malady, and the only solution was to attribute it to witchcraft. Someone must be fixed upon for the witch. To the surprise of everybody, a person of no less standing than my wife, Mary Parsons, was named the guilty person. Soon after the death of Mrs. Bartlett, her husband began to procure depositions made by neighbors against Mrs. Parsons, for the purpose of substantiating his accusations against her before the next court. Mrs. Parsons did not wait to be served with process, but appeared in person before the court to answer her accusers. In her plea she denied her guilt and asserted her own innocence, often mentioning how clear she was of such a crime and that the righteous God knew her innocence. But the court at Springfield decided to entertain the case and appointed a jury of chaste women to make diligent search upon the body of Mary Parsons, to find any marks of witchcraft. The indictment charged her with not having the fear of God before her eyes and entering into familiarity with the Devil. Mr. Hannum told of discontented words passed on both sides one March evening, and how the next morning a young and lusty cow lay in the yard ready to die, and did die a fortnight later, though he took great care of her night and day, giving her samp, pease, wholesome drinks, and eggs. Sarah Bridgman related how her eleven-year-old boy looking for cows in the swamp, fell over some logs and put his knee out of joint. The fracture was set, but the boy was in grievous torture for a month. One night he cried out and he said, "Goody Parsons sits on the shelf! Now she runs away and a black mouse follows her." After the matter was submitted to the jury in Boston, they brought in a verdict of *acquittal*. Thus ended the trial of Mary Parsons.

My Mary Parsons was *not* accused of witchcraft later that year when John Stebbins died at work in a sawmill. The logs and boards became bewitched and left hundreds of tiny spots on his body, as if made with small shot.

Nowicki flicks his spent cigarette on the lawn with a tiny move-
ment of the fingers—a gesture I am sure he learned from the
movies. His hair is done in the same style, thick with oil, pom-
padoured to a ridge on the forehead like a glacial fold of earth
in Poland. He is talking out of the side of his mouth to a colleague. Nowicki also works nights as a butcher over at the Stop
& Shop. He is proud to be a member of two unions, sorry to
be so close to retirement. I approach him the way I'd edge toward a barking dog, hand held palm down. "Where's Keefe?"
I ask. Nowicki sizes me up. It has been two weeks since Keefe
stopped showing up for work, midsummer, no prior warning.
Nowicki clearly has no desire to impart information I might
profit by. But he can't decide how I will use Keefe's where-
abouts to my advantage. It clearly pains him, weighing these
thoughts in the balance. He gives up. "Married," Nowicki
says. "Easthampton. Works at the felt factory. Lives two doors

down from me. Haven't seen him at the Majestic yet, but give him time. Wife goes to Smith." The Majestic is the X-rated movie theater in Easthampton. The fact that Keefe married a Smithie is another unexpected blow to the portrait I have been building of this man.

Northampton, Massachusetts flowers, and my garden calls
softly through open kitchen windows. Grape leaves yawn
open. The natural world asks of all its inhabitants only to act
naturally. But today a small package arrived at my post office
box on Pleasant Street, the neat brown paper untouched, yet
something about the smell of the glue was off, and I know I am
doomed. The contents of the package I won't mention, except
to say how fiercely happy they made me for ten minutes, and
then how sad, how bad they made me know I am. But I cannot
bring myself to destroy them. The rare trips to Northampton
Truman makes, the first thing he wants to do is spread them all
over the living room floor. I can name him—Truman Capote.
He was my lover, then my student, then my friend. We met at
the artist colony Yaddo. Now I am a caged creature he reveals
briefly to his fast friends. Last night he brought Cary Grant
and Lauren Bacall to my home, and when he made the slightest

move in the direction of my bedroom and the armoire where I've hidden the pictures of muscular naked men, I jumped out of my skin.

Beautiful Smith girls in white dresses walk single file down the path to Paradise Pond carrying Chinese lanterns, which they place on tiny barges and let float into the middle of the water. They brush past me tittering, alive with smells I ought to respond to, but my eye wanders to the gardener who digs a pit in the grass for the annual bonfire, sweat flying off his head like tears.

OCTOBER 1907
MOLLY BECK, 19

My name is Molly. I have worked at Judge Hammond's house for five years, since I left St. Michael's School. I clean bedrooms and sweep the halls and do laundry and sometimes I assist with dinners when guests are expected. Cook is a difficult woman who cannot convey her desires without losing track of her thoughts (and yet she expects me to know them anyway), but still I enjoy this duty most. I least enjoy opening up the house on Hammond Pond in Goshen mid-June. There are bears and mountain lions and bug-eyed owls that stare down at us from the hills, and we must keep the windows wide open for the airing out.

Tonight is a meeting of the People's Institute board. Judge Hammond won't say so but I know he dislikes the author Mr. George Washington Cable, who founded the benevolent organization. I like its annual flower show and competition—

town yards have noticeably improved since the competition began, my mother tells me. I would love to help out with the garden, but Cook jealously keeps that activity to herself. They say Mr. Cable came from New Orleans, but he sounds more like a Brooklyn man—my uncle Toby, for example, but I won't speak more of him.

Usually Mr. Cable excuses himself from dinner and places a telephone call to New York—can you imagine? I'm told he never pays for the call. I like the Secretary, Mr. Coolidge, even though he rarely says more than three words in succession. His kindly smile and his advice ("Go back to school") are always untouched by sternness or superiority. Others complain of his quiet. I do not feel the need for small talk with him, which is a relief. If I am alone in a room or hallway with Mr. Coolidge, I never worry about his thoughts. I do pity his lovely and talk-ative wife, who has to endure hours of silence and then the oc-casional compacted command—three orders reduced to one sentence. They say the Board of Directors values Mr. Coolidge for his hard work and because his notes of meetings are never more than a page long.

Judge Hammond lets Cook dictate the schedule of life around both houses too much, if you ask me, but since his wife died he prefers a woman for domestic decision-making. Cook gives Mr. Cable smaller portions of food, especially beef, and I do what I can to mask these displays of temper with potatoes and gravy and beans. Mr. Cable is not a genial man, as far as I can see, but one must give him credit for starting this institution. Reading a whole book gives me pain in the eyes, but I am told his books are not readable. He does not drink spirits or wine, so when the rest of the board becomes voluble, Mr. Cable sits back in his chair and watches. His stories of Civil War battles interest the room a great deal, but he prefers to tell us of the city of his birth, tales of commerce and mulattoes and yellow fever. I am glad I was born in Northampton, though I would like to have a house and garden of my own, but no husband, thank you very much.

My grandson and I drive to an abandoned house along the
Connecticut River, four miles from Geoffrey's parents' front
door. Directly above us is an equally abandoned railroad
bridge, which runs alongside the Coolidge Bridge. Across from
us is Elwell Island, a naturalist's wonderland. Both Geoff and
I are facing death. Geoffrey learned recently that his long-term
boyfriend is very ill with this awful new disease called AIDS.
For the time being, I seem to have beaten prostate cancer, but
I know better. Geoffrey spreads out the picnic on the rusty
metal table someone left here years before. He sets up the fold-
ing chairs for me and for himself, against the wind and facing
the Connecticut River. Beside us, to the north, is a hesitant
green band of the swamp in which we will go collecting. I walk
carefully from the car to my seat, and Geoff hands me one of
Elsie's famous chicken sandwiches, lots of pepper, butter, and
French bread. Geoff sits with his back to the table, legs kicked

out from the bench. The river gurgles and swirls and swells. The leaves are only just budding. I study the sandwich for some time, perhaps trying to retrieve a story from my memory, or maybe I'm worrying over my wife, whose memory is clearly failing. Geoff and I hold to a strict routine of talk and activity, which does not allow for soul-searching, but I think Geoffrey, at this moment, wants to ask me if I'm afraid of dying. My grandson isn't sure if he himself is. He opens his mouth, and I think I know what Geoff is about to say. We both breathe in the sweet smell of dirt warming in the first hot sun of the season.

*

The great poet Wallace Stevens and I walked halfway across the Coolidge Bridge over the Connecticut River, in Northampton, Massachusetts. It was a happy coincidence we were both in this handsome, dying mill town, he on business, me to meet my publisher in Cummington, a few miles up into the Berkshires. A white fog floated over the river. The steeples of Northampton flitted in and out of the moonlit mist. "There was a coup attempt at the company this week," Stevens said, of his long-time place of employment, The Hartford Accident and Indemnity Company. "Five of us stood behind the president, risking our jobs. We won. But today it dawned on me how close I came to losing this life, Bill, and I am shaken."

I said, "You always liked the job more than you let on to the art crowd we knew in our twenties. But the time is coming we will both have to retire to our rocking chairs." "No," Stevens said, with a catch in his throat. "I need the rhythm of office life. I prefer to break time down into six-minute segments. If I retired, Mrs. Stevens would get to know me and move back to Pennsylvania within the week. I don't think I could live a month without the smell of leather and coffee and cigarettes. The world of the office is more real than the world of Westerly Terrace. There's a different language for each department, a whole new climate and topography. If this war ever ends, I'm keen to see how the new breed of men changes the barometric pressure in the board rooms." I had never before heard so long a discourse on work from Wallace. I took Stevens' hand and kissed it. He gripped my shoulder as if he needed the help, and we walked slowly back to the car.

"We must see the Connecticut River where Jonathan Edwards cast out the devil," Stevens said. We drove, in a handsome Daimler, his driver Tex singing a show tune as he kept adjusting the rearview mirror. We followed the high ground away from Amherst, then dropped onto the flood plain, some of the best farmland in New England and the reason Northampton prospered in the seventeenth century, according to Stevens. We passed through a field, turned hard onto a dirt road, and came upon the river, the nose of the vehicle stopping just short of the black water. We climbed out of the car, amid damp, fertile smells, and the slope sent us up to our ankles in the current. Mosquitoes swarmed. Stevens unfurled himself and let fly a potent stream, which the insects followed down to the inky river. The moment Tex exposed himself, the mosquitoes lit on the soft flesh, and he shouted but could not stanch the natural course of events. Stevens said, "Your blood's too hot, young man. You must practice cool thoughts and cold feelings." "Or it might be that *your* circulation's not good, Wallace,"

I said, the doctor in me peeking out. Stevens waved his hand at my remark and made me fear briefly for the health of this friend, whom I'd thought was thawing out so beautifully at sixty-five.

"Drive," Stevens told his young colleague, giving detailed directions to a place wonderfully called Dryads Green. I asked if he'd been here before. Stevens said no, that he knew of the town only from a good map and a recent biography of a writer who used to live in Northampton—George Washington Cable. On Kensington Avenue, Stevens said, "We'll walk from here. Follow us in the car with your lights off." The driver laughed and obeyed. Large Victorian homes stood on the right, all dark, though the moonlight revealed charming living rooms through the picture windows, this ridiculous American style of presenting a false façade of happy home life to the public. Great elms arched overhead and threw shadows everywhere, some darker than others. I had been here alone, one block away, earlier in the evening.

"He was a New Orleans native," Stevens said, presumably of this George Washington Cable. "He was chased from the south for his frank views on intermarriage after the Civil War. He brought his family of daughters to Northampton because of Smith College. He knew town girls could attend the college free. Cable was notoriously cheap." We turned onto Dryads Green, the car rumbling happily behind us. The one street lamp spotlighted the yard and the front of the house Stevens thought George Washington Cable had built for his secretary. "Why are we looking at the secretary's home and not Cable's?" I asked. Stevens said, "Notice how sturdy the house is. You and I have worked most of our lives to build a similar solidity with our poetry and our day jobs, and this prose writer could also do it for his girlfriend."

Stevens and I returned to the Hotel Northampton, walking at a comfortable pace, the car motoring quietly behind us. Stevens cleared his throat.

"One bond many of us have," Stevens said, "is the memory of that golden hallway light when we were young and made to go to bed before we were ready. We lay there hearing laughter, music, mysterious sounds that would be silenced forever by the time we were older. When I stand in the dreary darkness of the stairwell I am more determined than ever to learn the secrets behind Elsie's door. You and that love of your life Florence cannot conceive it, I imagine, but Elsie and I have had separate bedrooms since the fourth night of our marriage. I creep up to the crack of light, hoping the floorboards will give my presence away, but they don't. On the long walk from the Canoe Club to Westerly Terrace, after two martinis, I ponder this marriage, the love drained out the way one empties the pipes in a cottage at the end of summer, for good reason, but it's sad nonetheless. Sometimes I hear her sigh when I'm stationed outside her bedroom. The fifteen years before Holly was born were not easy, nor happy, years. At least we were alone with our thoughts, both of us convinced our parents were right about the marriage, but too prideful to answer their critiques and allied only in that pride. I began to write poetry again when Holly was well into her early wisdom and Elsie had better possession of her moods and no longer claimed all ownership of the poems. Now I rise at daybreak, shave, etc. At six I start to exercise. At seven I massage and bathe. At eight I dabble with a therapeutic breakfast. From eight-thirty to nine-thirty I walk downtown, work all day…go to bed at nine. How I write poetry is something of a mystery. *Mon Dieu*, I am happy if I can find time to read a few lines, yours, Pound's, anybody's."

I was stunned by the intimacy of these revelations. No one who knew Stevens heard him speak of his wife—or himself for that matter—in any but the most general terms. I had met her on three occasions for only a few minutes at a time. She was beautiful and troubled, and as a doctor I saw the unmistakable evidence in both their behaviors of her quiet madness. I had always assumed Stevens protected her from the world. Now I understood he was protecting the two of them. This information would take many years to digest. My fingers, at that moment, happened to be separating a dime from pocket lint, and I was tempted to show Stevens the image of Elsie as she'd been in her youth, when she posed for Adolph Alexander Weinman as lady liberty.

A turquoise Volvo appeared on the long gravel road that snaked up the valley toward our country house. The car stopped at the cattle grate that my father had put in the year before he died (there were no cattle in the fields below their house, but Mother said he feared there *might* be one day). The backseat door on the driver's side opened. A small suitcase tumbled out. A boy my own age climbed down. "Don't bother getting out, Father," the boy said. I could not see the face of the father. I was in shadow, behind a rose of Sharon bush, a dozen feet away. No one was expected. Mother was running errands in Northampton. I did not recognize this car or the boy who had arrived in it. Shyness kept me momentarily out of sight, and when I recovered my manners, the Volvo was kicking up stones and speeding down the hill. The boy walked directly to my hiding place and said, "Your mother told my father I could spend the weekend."

The boy would not give his name, so we chose one for him, Sylvester, from Sylvester Graham, inventor of the Graham Cracker, who lived in Northampton a long time ago. Sylvester did not reject his name. He asked, every once in a while, where my mother was. He said it was not wise to leave such young children alone in the wild like this. We gave Mother a certain amount a freedom after Father and Robert Kennedy died, which happened the same weekend. This weekend was quiet. We had a lunch of watercress sandwiches, which were actually dandelion and peanut butter sandwiches, and then Sylvester asked if he could call someone. He picked up the phone on the nightstand next to our parents' bed, and he dialed a number he appeared to know. We wanted to know who Sylvester was calling. "My best friend, Brian Kiteley," he answered, with great confidence. "My mother ran away with an Italian professor," he said. "We moved a month ago, because Father could not bear the memories in our old house." One of the twins wanted to know if he was a professor of Italian or an *Italian* professor—a good question for a six-year-old. When no one answered at the Kiteleys, Sylvester began to cry. We escorted him out to the screened-in porch, the addition to the house our father had just finished, when he had his heart attack. We used this airy room only on special occasions. The rest of the house was 200 years old and warped and sloping, which we liked. This room had a cement floor. It got very chilly on August nights, and bugs bounced off the screen. Sylvester calmed down after we gave him a candy cigar and the best chair in the house. The sky was clouding over again. It was late afternoon. The twins stood up and walked to the screen door. I went to see where they were going, and I saw them crawling under the fence that was the shortcut to the well. "Come with me," I told Sylvester.

We came to the fence. Sylvester looked down at me. I was crouching to slide under the fence. He clearly was not going to follow. I shimmied on my back, head first, down the opening the twins and I had made. I ran toward the old well, which was one hundred feet from the house, and I heard a siren. Flashing lights reflected off the sumac stand, which was already turning bright red. I hoisted myself up to the rim of the well, and one brilliant flash of lightning revealed dozens of yards of the well. The twins were nowhere to be seen, but I also knew, as if I'd known all my life, that they had fallen down deep into this hole. I saw two policemen setting out across the overgrown croquet pitch in my direction, but they scattered and retreated at the next flash of lightning. It began to rain.

One moment there was a loud buzzing sound behind me. The next moment I was lying on the couch in the screened-in porch. My feet were not allowed on the couch, but I couldn't make them move. A policeman said his name was Arlin, loosened his tie, and asked where my father was. "He died of a massive coronary last June," I said, repeating the sentence Mother had used for months. The policeman winced, as if the news weren't over a year old. He asked if I had any relatives nearby. My big toe twitched but I said I couldn't remember. The policeman said, "I have some very sad news for you." The twins are hurt, my panicked mind shouted. But the policeman said, "Your mother was in an accident." My relief that the twins were unharmed made me laugh. The policeman looked as if he'd just eaten one of the bitter peanuts you get in a bag of peanuts. He left the room, but I could hear whispering in the kitchen. A slow rusty creak meant the screen door was opening. The familiar noise of the twins' mouth breathing, after they'd been running, gave me a sloppy, happy feeling. The two policemen were asking someone his name, and Sylvester said, "My name is John Gathers, Jr. My father is John Gathers, on Henshaw Avenue in Northampton. I'm sorry I can't remember our phone number. We just moved there."

The twins started crying as soon as they saw the policemen. The last time they saw men in uniforms our father had died. I felt weary and there was an odd burnt smell. I still could not move my hands or legs very much. A face appeared above me, too close to my forehead. It was this John Gathers, Jr. "Since your mother has died, maybe you can come and live with us," he said. For an instant, I had a picture in my mind, complete with the odor of a strange but appealing house, another home on Henshaw Avenue, where my father sometimes swung on the swing at backyard parties. I did not mind the idea of moving into this house, even if I did not like the two older boys who tended to pick me up and carry me around back and tickle my underpants. But moving was out of the question. Mother had enough on her hands, renting out the third floor of the Northampton house to guests, keeping the Monday Club going all by herself, and looking after her rambunctious children. A wave of calm overtook me. The room grew dark. A candle I had not noticed before flickered and the air cooled. The combination of chill and irregular light made me sleepy and thoughtless. When I opened my eyes again the twins were playing chess.

I did not fall in love with the Northampton Association at first sight, for I arrived there when appearances did not correspond with the large ideas of the Association. The other utopian communities of Brook Farm and Fruitlands did not draw me to them. A silk factory provided labor and sustenance for the Northampton Association, but they were wanting in means to carry out their ideas of beauty and elegance. I thought I would stay with them one night. But literary and refined persons were living in that simple manner and submitting to the privations such an infant institution ought to have, and I said, "Well, if these can live here, *I* can." I gradually became attached to the place and the people. It was no small thing to have found a home in a community composed of some of the choicest spirits of the age, where all was characterized by an equality of feeling, a liberty of thought and speech, and a largeness of soul I had not come upon before, in any of my wanderings.

When they first saw me, I would not be induced to take regular wages, believing that Providence had provided me with a never-failing fount, from which my every want might be perpetually supplied through my mortal life. In this, I had calculated too fast. The Associationists soon found it most expedient to act individually, and the subject of this sketch found her dreams unreal. I myself flung back upon my own resources for the supply of my needs. Slavery, hard labor, and exposure had made sad inroads on my iron constitution, inducing chronic disease and premature old age. I washed clothes and sang my own hymns to the hundred members at night, spoke my native Dutch tongue to amuse children. I heard the secretary boast, "We cultivate a farm, we sell lumber and shingles, we grow silk and manufacture it. We have amongst us teachers for the instruction of our children, blacksmiths, carpenters, masons, and shoemakers. But we need a wheelwright, a machinist, a bootmaker, and a baker." Discontented souls all over the world yearn for a taste of Utopia, a yearning most intense in those who have not succeeded in ordinary life, either because of temperament or plain incompetence. But I soon yearned for a home of my own, a "house," and I was able to procure one at 35 Park Street, in Florence, where I have lived for seven years now.

From time to time I visit the Bridge Street home of Seth Hunt, treasurer of the Connecticut River Railroad and a free thinker. It is said his home is a stop on the Underground Railroad, which I will neither confirm nor deny. I begin to travel and speak to large and small groups. I am not an orator, but I am told I can keep a crowd in unison with my thoughts and prayers. To my great surprise, this has become a calling, and I enjoy talking to the soul of a gathering of people, not the individuals but the collection of their good deeds and desires.

JULY 1954
ERIC KITELEY, 52
THE DEAD MAN SWITCH

My teenage son Gary flew over the great rock in the middle of
the island in 1954, and he decided on another way of describing its shape: a mechanic bent under the hood of a Nash. The
original was a bear scooping ants from a tree stump and so the
name, Hungry Bear Island. The families left Monday afternoon
in three cars. Our company float plane, flying in later this clear
Tuesday morning from Saskatoon, will take me east to Mani-
toba wheat fields threatened by an outbreak of angry rust. My
wife's sister was once known for her love of rough camping
and bushwhacking in this area, before they built on the land.
She said she never realized how boring cabin life could be until
she stopped roughing it. We had four games of cribbage going
at once, the kitchen cabin open till midnight, fiddling contests
in the "square," railroad stories about mountain lions in trees
overhanging the tracks from my sister-in-law's husband Bill.
Still, she would periodically poke me in the side. "I'm losing my

mind. There's nothing to do."

I have a soft spot for this sister-in-law, Lena. When we moved to Minneapolis, she took in my younger son so he could finish his last year of high school in Saskatoon. Now that he was in college she was full of wisdom. "If you ask me, I'd make him stop flying," she said five or six times. "Men and their machines. When my Bill was young you could see it in his eyes—he fell in love with me on a train. Now look at him—he's dying out along with his beloved steam locomotives. He says he can't stand the new dead man switch on the diesels." I wanted to make a joke about dying out and dead man switches, but I could not come up with one. "The next war Gary will be drafted," she continued. "This Eisenhower is bound to want to fight again. Stalin, or whoever's in charge over there, is likely exterminating more Jews or Armenians—wonderful people. Do you know my new butcher Danny?" My other son had been rescued from disgrace in Lena's eyes when he decided not to become a minister. My wife's sisters had a running argument over ostentatious Christianity, which Lena detested. "I don't tell people how to do their business," she said. We all knew what she meant. "Teaching at university is good," she said, about my older son, who was doing a PhD in Minnesota. "You keep up with things. Science doesn't pass you by. You're not obsolete at sixty like Bill and me. Of course, he'll come up to the University of Saskatchewan when he's done, won't he?"

The sisters, especially my wife Elsie, worried Lena was losing her mind. In their cabin kitchens they would grill each other. "She's getting so crotchety," one would say. She was always crotchety, I'd respond. "She talks all this cracked politics and antireligious tripe." I'd remind them that she had never gone to church, preferring Sunday hikes, and she had hated every prime minister and American president since Coolidge. "She doesn't go camping anymore." There, I pointed out, was the problem. "Unlike all of you, she's getting old." "Oh Eric," they said in unison.

After the Americans had won at Trenton, a victorious Major Seth Pomeroy called at my house on Pudding Lane in Northampton, Massachusetts. He wore his gorgeous red cloak, and he broke in on me. I was drunk with despondency. Pomeroy cried, "Wake up, you cowardly skunk, the day is ours!" I laughed and for a moment the sun shone again. We walked through town and up to Round Hill, exchanging gossip and charting the progress of the war against the English. At the summit, I lost all my air. I sat on a stump weeping. "We will all be executed. We have overstepped our authority. Canada is lost." Pomeroy tried to cheer me to no avail. He took off his cloak and wrapped my shivering shoulders in it, and then, hoisted me up in his arms. He said he was surprised by how light I had become. We descended. I am ashamed to say I whimpered now and again, but I also issued orders and suggestions for reorganizing the militias. Pomeroy, who did not trust his own memory, asked me to repeat the orders many times. In minutes, the curious sight of a seventy-year-old man carrying a fifty-three-year-old man in his arms, two River Gods no less, gathered a crowd. Pomeroy asked this man and that to store specific bits of my instructions. These blasted fits of melancholy have kept me from what would have been my duties in the Congress. At the First Church, a great blacksmith took me in his arms and delivered me to Pudding Lane. Seth Pomeroy declined the command of Brigadier General. When news reached the town that he had died in Peekskill, New York, we all mourned. In particular, I recall the strength of his arms carrying me, but I might be thinking of the blacksmith's arms.

I took my sister-in-law Lena out beetle collecting with me the last day at Christopher Lake. Lena asked me why I still worked for Robin Hood Flour—I'm a cereal chemist. "Can't you do the entomology full-time?" she wondered. I found the idea very amusing, and Lena decided she couldn't stand to see me rooting about in tree trunks like a common bear, so she turned back. I was in the forest bog, east of the lake, when I smelled diesel. A little farther on, I heard the idling engine. The sound was steady when I stood still. It did not grow or weaken. I knew only railroad tracks crossed this bog, but a locomotive would not make such sounds unless stationary. Sure enough, through the woods, I spotted the gleaming metal. The cabin light was on, trees hung over the lone engine. The sight was startling. I'd ridden plenty of locomotives with Lena's husband, Bill. I had spent enough time in railroad yards. But here was an unfamiliar sight: a train in its natural setting. I called out for the engineer. I climbed into the driver's cab and fingered the radio dials, thinking of calling for help. The nearest town was five miles away, the nearest people in our own cabins halfway across the lake. "Hey you," a voice shouted. "Outta my train." I turned to see Bill stumbling up the small grade to the tracks, buttoning his fly. "Oh Eric, it's you." We shook hands. I was very glad to see him again. We had already said goodbye once that day. I'd forgotten he was transferring the engine north. He had driven up in it Friday and left it ten miles south of the lake at a yard. "Had to pee," he said. "Came on me all of a sudden like a news flash." I asked to see the famous dead man switch. Bill said, "A device designed by executives in Montreal to torture engineers." If you release the pressure, the current is cut off, I asked, and the brakes are applied automatically? "By force of death, instant illness, or urinary necessity," Bill said, laughing.

"Grampa," my second grandson, Brian, says, in the darkness. I am confused and worried. "You're in Northampton, Massachusetts," he says. I feel around me, worn cotton sheets, a soft corduroy bedcover the family used for the children, who are all grown now, like this young man. I want to refute my grandson's statement, but the evidence is against me. "You were talking in your sleep," he says. "You said something about Calvin Coolidge. Want to hear a story? When he was just starting out as a lawyer, Cal used to go to Rahar's for lunch every day. Rahar's is still on Crafts Avenue, you know. He ordered the same meal and same whiskey for lunch, every time. One day there was a sign, over the bar. 'Second well drink free,' it said. He had his same lunch and one drink, then went back to work. After work he returned to Rahar's and sat down at the bar and said, 'I'll have that second drink now.' What I love about this story is that Calvin Coolidge had a whiskey for lunch every day."

I laugh, appreciating this young storyteller's desire to talk me out of my terror. My grandson is writing a novel about me, and he enjoys asking about ancient history, as he rarely did when he was growing up. I was startlingly clearly back at Christopher Lake, Saskatchewan in 1954. It *is* of course December 1985. I have cancer, but I can't die. My wife Elsie, I find more and more evidence of this, will be unable to cope without me.

"What was the dream about?" the twenty-nine-year-old asks. I wait a moment for my head to clear. I am drenched with sweat. I arrange my pillows behind me. I tell my grandson I was recalling a trip to Christopher Lake. I remind him who Lena and Bill were, and he chuckles at me for thinking he wouldn't know them. I tell my grandson that this "dream" was unusual because it got a few of the details wrong. Why would I be able to remember the past so well and yet not know my younger son was not the one who stayed behind with Lena and Bill? It was my elder son, this boy's father, who stayed with Lena and Bill. Also, Bill never drove diesels. He was retired along with his beloved steam engines. What was the purpose of these easily recognizable flaws in the story? My grandson says, "Maybe you wanted to know it was a dream, so you could enjoy the experience more. If it were a pure return to that time, how would you be able to savor the sensations?"

My grandson continues talking, despite having exposed this lovely revelation to me—he should stop to savor it himself, but he can't know how he is affecting me. He is telling me stories from my past, which he does well now, although he has difficulty keeping straight the fictions he is writing and the facts he has gleaned from my own probably inaccurate stories. I cannot concentrate on his voice.

Lena did become mentally deranged, within a dozen years, and in retrospect we all saw the evidence years before. I worry now that I won't have the courage to tell my sons about Elsie. Bill died in 1967, and really life was never the same after that. I am glad to be with this grandson, but that trip to Christopher Lake was a time free of pain and worry when I climbed up into Bill's engine and saw him buttoning his fly. I rarely feel nostalgia for places. People and places intertwined will do it to me. I miss Bill and Lena terribly, but I see that it is my own impending death and Elsie being stranded in the world without my help that worries me, in this dream. I don't mean that I am so important to her well-being. But she is deteriorating, her memory failing, her soul dwindling away little by little, and I have been hiding her condition from my sons as best I can.

I try to pay attention to my grandson, who is saying something else, but I can't keep track of the words. His young face shows concern, embarrassment, and distraction, all ordinary feelings for someone in his position. I stand unsteadily. I walk toward the bathroom. I need to pee, and this makes me think happily of Bill in the woods. I reach for the doorknob. I believe I took the train through this town in 1933. The tracks from Montreal come down the river valley, which opens up south of the Vermont-Massachusetts border. It was fall, brilliant golds and red. The spires of the town appeared before anything else. I was sitting on the side opposite the river, watching the hills to the west slide by, listening to an old farmer from White River Junction talk about milk prices. I opened the window before we reached the station along Pleasant Street. The smell of fermenting leaves and apples overpowered the farmer and me. He stopped talking. A moment ago, I think my grandson said, "Don't open the window. It's below zero." I disagree, but he is still among the living, and this gives him a certain amount of authority.

DECEMBER 1943
MATHIAS WEEKS, 28
THE COOLIDGE BRIDGE

I don't know much about gods, but I think the river is a brown god—sullen, untamed, untrustworthy, and, in the end, just a riddle for builders of bridges. My job was to hammer the hot rivets into the support beams of the new bridge, following the orders of men who were also following orders. We took our lunches on the I beams, even when there was no platform under us. The Connecticut River in May is a syrup, sluggish and hypnotic. My mate Sabin, the one man who died while we were building the bridge, often fell asleep at lunch, dangling fifty feet above water (not a fatal plunge), jerking awake with bad dreams about his sister and her boyfriend. He died on solid earth, when someone dropped a pail of box-end wrenches on his head. I did not know I could get used to such dying. When we trained for our bombing runs in New Jersey and then in Hampshire, we lost four planes and all but three of the crew men. It was a relief to be in combat, in some ways. You knew you were going to die. Training missions wasted our anxiety muscles. There was a moment, before the shrapnel ripped me apart, when I thought I was on the nearly completed Coolidge Bridge. Gusts of sweet river air, unfastened from the dream of life. I awoke to black flak and Messerschmitt 109s. They washed me out of the turret with a hose.

Barbara, Geoffrey, and I flew up the Connecticut River on Christmas Eve. My sister Barb was our pilot. This was the first flight she could take passengers, after she got her pilot's license. We imagined our parents staring up at the sky, all three of their children in a single-engine plane several thousand feet off the ground. I felt utterly at ease the moment the landing gear left the runway—my little sister flying us around the neighborhood. We flew over the Quabbin Reservoir to the east of Amherst, Boston's drinking water. It was such cold clear air, and absolutely windless, that we could see to the depths of the reservoir the old towns sunk forever by the flooding of their valleys in the 1930s. None of us spoke, as Barbara banked the plane so we could peer more intently into the past. All that remained of the town of Enfield was its roads, ghostly in the shimmering depths. We flew farther down the valley and spied a road that dipped into the water, where the reservoir was shallow, so the road continued underwater and came up on the other side. Geoffrey asked Barbara to fly over our home on the way back to the little landing strip called LaFleur Airport. The house was visible from 3,000 feet. Just a short distance from Harrison Avenue was the Mill River's forested ravine, even in winter a lush wilderness that crept up to the town's manicured lawns and right angles. We followed Elm Street to the downtown area, then Bridge Street back to the airport.

JULY 1958

SYLVIA PLATH, 25

We are recovering from a week of the bird, which we found near death on our windowsill. We killed it. Ted fixed a rubber bath hose to the gas jet on the stove and taped the other end to a cardboard box. I could not look. I cried and cried. We were desperate to get the sickly little bird off our necks, miserable at its persistent pluck and sweet temper. I looked in. Ted took the bird out of the box too soon, and it lay in his hand on its back, opening and shutting its beak with effort and waving its upturned feet. Five minutes later he brought the bird to me, perfect and beautiful in death. Born July 2, 1958 (we guess). Dead July 15, 1958. Northampton, Massachusetts.

We walk in the dark blue night of Child's Park, lift a druid stone, dig a hole in its crater, bury the bird, and roll the stone back. We place ferns and a green firefly on the grave. I have a pair of silver-plated scissors in my raincoat pocket to cut another rose—yellow, if possible—from the rose garden (by the stone lion's head fountain). I want a rose to unbud. The almost-black red rose in our living room is now exhaling a prodigal scent that means it will soon die. We stroll on the road to the stucco house and descend to the rose garden. We hear a loud crackling sound, the breaking of twigs. We think it's a man we saw in another part of the park coming through the thick rhododendron groves from the frog pond. The yellow roses are blowsy, blasted, no bud in view. I lean to snip a pink uncurling bud, and three hulking girls come out of the rhododendron grove, sheepish and hunched in light manila-colored raincoats. We stand regnant in our rose garden and stare them down. They shamble whispering to the formal garden of white peonies and red geraniums, and they are at a loss under a white arbor. "I'll bet they're waiting to steal some flowers," Ted says, as we are doing. Eventually the girls walk off. I see an orange rosebud I've never seen before and bend to clip it, a bud of ginger silk. The gray sky lowers, thunder rumbles in the pines, and a warm soft rain begins to fall as if gently squeezed from a gray sponge.

Truman Capote is visiting my teacher and now colleague Newton Arvin this weekend. Truman is a baby boy, though he must be in his middle thirties. He has a big head, like a prematurely delivered infant, a tall white forehead, a little drawstring mouth, a shock of blond hair, a mincing skipping fairy gait, a black velvet jacket. Ted and the other men hate the homosexual part of him with more than their usual fury. But there is something else that bothers them: jealousy at his success. If he weren't successful there would be nothing to be angry about. I am moved and amused. My stitches pull and snick.

Truman tells me in the Renaissance there was an opinion that the plague might be distinguished by breathing upon a mirror. Breath condensed and living creatures might be seen by a microscope—monstrous and frightful shapes, creatures a cross between slugs and dragons. Truman likes this notion of early scientific discovery mixed with gothic fantasy. They did not know what they were looking for, although they were going in the right direction centuries before bacteria and viruses were discovered. Truman claims a great deal can be learned of a man if he breathes on a mirror. I laugh at this, saying it is hard to imagine Ted ever getting that close to his own image. Truman says he's seen Ted looking in plenty of mirrors in just the hour he's known him. Is this true? Is Truman pulling my leg? Does it matter? I am briefly happy.

Truman sees something in me, or else my former teacher Newton has spoken well of me to him. He says he wants to rescue me from my "hypermasculine" men, and we set out to visit a bar in Easthampton. I drive, because neither Truman nor Newton know how to. The bar is full of like-minded men, and I am the only woman, the smoke ropy, the floor covered with the crackling skin of dead insects. I call Ted from the phone booth to say where we are, and he is nonchalant, disdainful, happy to be free of me for a couple of hours. I remind him of a particular sexual position he likes me to be in, and he is silent. Then he hangs up. This leaves me more than usually unsettled and sexually transparent. At the booth, Newton asks me how I like teaching at Smith—I was hired last fall. The lectures mortify me, the grading is endless, the students' minds are like pudding, but I tell Newton Ted and I are ecstatic, which is true some of the time.

Later, I wait for a lull in the conversation, which I find is rare with Truman, but one lull does arrive, and I ask them to describe homosexual sexual activities to me. Newton goes cold and he fixes his face in a hard stare, but Truman laughs and laughs. He paints very precise anatomical studies in the air, with one wan finger drawing the imaginary scenes and positions. Slowly Newton's face resettles and he joins in the talk. I get much more than I expect, and it is my turn to feel my face go rigid and unsmiling, but gradually I too find humor in the complicated maneuvers. I ask if they get bored with each other, one always the actor, while the other was acted upon? Even Truman becomes quiet at this question. Newton finally speaks. He says the horror of their status and situation makes them refugees with each other, and they find solace in each others' arms. Truman bursts out laughing. We turn to other men, Truman says, many other men, to stave off the boredom, even my donnish Newton Arvin here. Arvin does not deny the assertion. I choose that moment to visit the powder room, but I discover it is occupied by several men. I return to the booth and ask the boys if they mind me taking them home. I am tired. Truman seems to have moved into the booth permanently while I was away, stretched out like The Nude Maja. He says they'll call a cab for themselves, but thanks anyway.

Chastened, I drive the leafy hilly roads back to Elm Street and our empty apartment.

My father and I are talking about a colleague of his who just committed suicide. The man brought a canister of compressed carbon dioxide home with him from the lab (he taught chemistry). He did it in his car, windows shut tight, doors to the garage closed. The carbon dioxide suffocated him—a quick, grisly death. Murray and I are making dinner out of the barest ingredients, because Murray and Jean never keep much in their fridge or pantry. I find two cans of whole tomatoes. I instruct my father to get the sherry I saw in their liquor cabinet. They do have fairly fresh cream, maybe because Barb visited recently (she uses it in her coffee). I smash and dice garlic. I find a few shallots in good condition in the onion cabinet. Jean has been in Boston for three days doing something for the League of Women's Voters. Murray has clearly let things slide, but he remembers he has some chicken stock frozen, which has a label saying "Feb 1985." We heat it, and the aroma that comes off the trickles of liquid is quite pleasant, comfortingly familiar. I chop the shallots and sauté them in butter. I realize that we are not talking, so I throw out a phrase or two about the suicide, I forget exactly what, something to the effect that I'd like to go that way too, before AIDS catches up with me. Murray laughs. The tomato soup will be ready in fifteen minutes. We set the timer on the simmering liquid and take the sherries I poured to the front porch so we can enjoy the evening sun. Are you upset by the suicide? I ask, settling into the rusted lawn chair. Jan Hemminger is weeding across the street, on her knees and facing away from us, but she calls out hello to Murray, who shouts back a joke about peonies and ants. Murray returns his attention to me. "Yes, I've found myself thinking about the way he did it, more than the fact that he did it. We were close. Part of a group that met once a month to talk science and philosophy and ethics. No one saw it coming. I had lunch with him two days ago, and I did not notice the slightest hint of sadness. Stanley Rothman stopped by my office after he'd heard the news. He was confounded. 'Why would he do it? He had everything—perhaps he had too much.' Stan told a story about a young medical student who had just finished his didactic therapy at McLean Hospital outside Boston. This meant he was set to become a therapist. The profession no longer condoned therapists who had crippling neuroses themselves. Theoretically, then, this fellow was a mentally healthy man, ready to help other people find their way toward mental health. He showed no signs of depression or crippling neuroses. He committed suicide several days after his didactic therapy ended." I tell my father I think one cannot read the mind of a potential suicide, even moments before the act. Murray stands up abruptly, departs for the kitchen, turns off the buzzer, which I did not hear, and returns with the bottle of sherry. He pours

148

us both slightly more than he poured the first time. We drink in silence. Murray drums his fingers on the metal table. Jan calls out, from across the street, "Do you boys want to join us for dinner?" Murray replies, "We just made a soup, but thanks." "Come for dessert then. I know Jean won't be back for another day. I have Boston cream pie." We hear whistling for a few moments, a tune from *Man of La Mancha*. Then a screen door squeak indicates Jan has gone inside her house. The sherry is good. The soup is better.

Three or four of my brothers killed themselves—we can't be sure of the fourth. Adolf Hitler and I attended the same primary school in Linz for two years, but I rarely looked up from my shoes. Music flowed through our home the way blood flows through a good heart, and the last composer of any note was Labor. Of my illustrious (if suicidal) family, I was the last and least talented. My only skill was the ability to hide pain— who knows someone else's pain, anyway? I find myself now in America, to which my father ran away when he was a boy. He stayed two years, playing piano, inventing a photographic repro-duction technique, digging a subway tunnel. When he returned, his father relented and let him study engineering, which he'd insisted was no profession for a gentleman before my father escaped to America. I experience on this side of the Atlantic something like my father's excitement. A former student of mine who once betrayed me hosts me here in Northampton.

I am dying, so I don't recall the specifics of her betrayal. Alice takes me to the Aqua Vitae restaurant. We eat clams, which I can hold down. In passing, she mentions how old the town is. I tell the story of a student who visited Cairo and saw Roman ruins there. He said they looked brand new, compared to the Pharaonic monuments.

I went to Cambridge at the deepest part of the Depression, and three years later I returned to the United States with few prospects for a teaching position. One of my advisers, Ludwig Wittgenstein, was aware of this, and he offered to help me with my PhD thesis. G. E. Moore had accepted both parts of a paper, which constituted part of the dissertation, and he had already published Part I in his journal *Mind*. This paper drew heavily on what I thought I had learned from Wittgenstein in my course with him. When Wittgenstein saw it, he felt his views were not properly represented and said the book was not yet ready for publication. He advised withdrawal of Part II. There was disagreement over this, although I did not question that Wittgenstein was in the best position to know whether his views had been properly represented. In Wittgenstein's class two other students and I had taken notes, which became *The Blue Book*. In the end, there was a break between Wittgenstein and me, and dictation of a second manuscript, *The Brown Book,* ceased. I never had the slightest doubt that what Wittgenstein wanted to say was very important. It was a burden to feel responsible for the cessation of a piece of work. I saw him once more, for a lunch at my flat on the day I left Cambridge.

I recall arriving in Northampton the first time, coming up by train from New Haven. The train passed directly underneath Mount Tom, on the west side of the river, and we came out of this mountain shade late in the day to the unreal brightness of the wide valley. I was alone, having lost my position at the University of Michigan because the department felt that it did not require the services of a woman professor after all (I taught there for one year). My husband Morris would not arrive here for another year. I loved the town from the first. I stepped into the fairly elaborate train station, and a lady taxi driver took me up Elm Street to the apartment building where I stayed. It was not a city, but it had a bustle one associates with much larger towns. All of the senses were engaged those first weeks I lived here—beautiful colors very early that year, apples rotting on the ground, Smithies serenading me with exquisite songs whenever I passed nearby Haven House, even the touch of the banister in Seelye Hall, where the department was housed then—like a stone worn smooth by eons of surf.

Wittgenstein and I patched things up. I know you want me to say something about Wittgenstein other than the merely philosophical. I did not watch for anything else from him. I am a woman, so I did not receive invitations to the westerns and film noirs he loved. With me it was tea, sedate conversation, all the lights on bright, to his liking. He came to Northampton once, and he asked to visit the model farm at the Vocational

Technical School. He particularly enjoyed the milking machines they were designing then. He asked the teacher who gave us the tour many acute questions, and when we were done, the teacher took me aside and wanted to know what branch of the Agriculture Department Mr. Wittgenstein was in.

Wittgenstein was not what you would call a friendly man, except for his generosity of spirit, his keen interest in one's thoughts, and his loyalty to his friends. But he unsettled most everyone he met with deep and penetrating questions. One was constantly on one's toes around him. They were generally good questions, but the most intelligent and respectable of targets for these questions felt slighted by them. He did not respect a reputation previous to the moment, and this never failed to offend people with reputations for intelligence. Yes, he seemed to respect me, but I have to say he rarely really saw me. I asked good questions, he once said, and that was the highest compliment he could pay. Was I in love with him? What a question. I loved his mind.

SEPTEMBER 1989
BRIAN KITELEY, 32

Some Northampton street names: First Square, Fourth, Fifth, Paradise, Florence, Bliss, Young Rainbow, Old Rainbow, Fairfield, Fern, Locust, Myrtle, Maple, Elm, Audubon, Evergreen, Woodlawn, Dryads Green, Spring, Linden, Walnut, Olive, Cherry, Orchard, Lawn, Cooke, Fruit, Burts Pit, Swan, Riverside, Rust, North Farms, West Farms, Mt. Tom, Rocky Hill, South Pynchon Meadow, Meadow, Swamp, Nook, Curtis Nook, King, Kings, Gothic, Chapel, Fort, Pilgrim, Stoddard, Lyman, Parsons, Edwards, Pomeroy, Hawley, Forbes, Trumbull, Munroe, Calvin, West, Old Ferry, Bridge, Crescent, Prospect, Upland, Hillside, Lexington, Franklin, Washington, Madison, Harrison, Garfield, Taylor, Winter, Summer, Sumner, Lincoln, Grant, Northern, Sherman, Union, Graves, Liberty, Texas, Coolidge, Wilson, Kensington, Maynard, Jewell, Pearl, Green, Federal, Main, Front, Center, Market, Fort Hill, Cosmian, Masonic, Corticelli, Dickinson, Whittier, Ellington,

Hollywood, Gleason, Ahwaga, Massasoit, Nonotuck.

Nonotuck was the name of the Indian settlement before it was called Northampton. Massasoit means leader of leaders, head of a confederacy of Indian tribes—the Wampanoags, Nipmucks, Pocumptucks, Nahigansetts, and Massachusetts. The man who was Massasoit in 1621 hosted the Pilgrims at Plymouth for the first Thanksgiving. Massasoit Street sits tidily between Woodlawn Avenue and Franklin Street, bordered by Elm and Prospect Streets. Calvin Coolidge lived for years in a duplex on Massasoit Street, before and after his presidency. My family lived on South Street for two years, then on Harrison Avenue, one house down from what long ago had been Judge Hammond's house, on the corner of Harrison Avenue and Elm Street. Judge Hammond was Calvin Coolidge's boss many years back. When I was in high school, the crowd I hung out with was called the Elm Street crowd, meaning we were generally related to Smith College, which was two blocks from our house. I knew the town as a pedestrian when I lived there as a child and teenager, so my worldview was limited. I did not learn to drive until college. It's a confusing town, the main roads meandering this way and that, following ancient cow paths. The Connecticut River is generally to the east, but it's also to the north and south, because of a great sweeping curve. The big hills gently rise to the west—the Berkshires—but the only visible hills are south and southeast—Mt. Tom and Mt. Holyoke. The village of Florence, so named because of its nineteenth-century silk manufacturing, is uphill and west, and Leeds is even farther west. I used to say that I never knew directions until my parents had south-facing solar energy panels placed on the roof of our second-floor front porch—it is a densely forested hilly town, so sunsets half the year are mysteriously diffused. The town's area is large, ten miles east to west, and six or seven miles north to south, but its population remained stable and small during my childhood, around 30,000, and it has grown very little since then.

My new husband, Mr. Jonathan Edwards, and I traveled together to our new home along the Connecticut, a shining river.
Sloops carried sugar, rum, molasses, and iron from the Long
Island Sound upriver. A trail worn smooth and wide enough for
oxcarts followed the water. Just beyond Wethersfield, known
for its onion beds and pretty girls, we came to the lively port of
Hartford, where vessels sometimes lined up three deep at the
wharves. Nearby, in East Windsor, my husband's parents provided a comfortable stopping place. Beyond Hartford the river
was too tricky for sloops, so traffic was transferred to clumsy
flatboats poled by husky men. At Longmeadow the river was its
widest—2,100 feet between its banks—then it closed upon a
gorge and a falls at South Hadley. Now the smell of wilderness
was on the left of the horseback rider, coming from tangles of
wild grapes, raspberries, plums, bayberries, and currants. The
weather that fall swung to alarming extremes. In September

there were unusually high winds. On October 29 an earthquake terrified New England with flashes of bluish flames running along the ground. In spite of the weird weather, work on the house continued. Mr. Edwards, recalling the elms of New Haven, planted one on his own lawn. I concerned myself with the kitchen and the garden, and I read the first sermon Pastor Edwards would deliver.

The boot of the Japanese soldier kicked the trunk of a palm tree, and a handful of small cocoanuts rained down. I crawled along the sand to my enemy. I felt no pain at the moment, but it was coming in excruciating waves. A giant green beetle clung to the cheek of the Japanese soldier, looking like an extension of his helmet. I flicked the beetle off, and the man I'd been shooting at moments ago said, "Thank you. This insect appeared to be eating me, and I don't think I'm dead yet." I sat carefully against the palm tree. These words spoken seemed to hang in the air like a mist. Were they truly English words? Was I hallucinating? Was I dead? The Japanese soldier's speech sounded to my Western Massachusetts ears like a Boston-Harvard accent, burnished and self-satisfied. The Japanese spoke again: "My name's Sam. Forgive me for firing on you. Are you hit? I think I'm done for."

I did not answer. We stared at each other for a long while. I said, at last, "I am Tom Andrews. I grew up in Northampton, Massachusetts. I'm a hemophiliac. I was able to lie easily enough to the army medical people in Holyoke (fifteen miles from Northampton), and I qualified for officer training. My older brother died a few years ago, oddly of another blood disease exactly the opposite of mine. I think I'm hit pretty bad, too, but I have to say it's a relief to bleed out. When I bump my knee against a coffee table, I can bleed inside for hours. You wouldn't believe how painful that is."

Sam examined my wounds, which were on my thigh and on the left side of my stomach. He said, "Funny. I think we will both die, and our men have clearly moved on. I don't know how long I passed out. Gut wounds can take days to kill you. I attended MIT, by the way. I visited your town a few times, to date a good Japanese girl who attended Smith College. Northampton impressed me as a sort of Eden. I wonder if we ever walked past each other on the streets there." I asked if he married the good Japanese girl. Sam said no; she was much higher born than him. She was willing to date in the US, but she made it clear that they could not continue their relations back in Japan. Her father was the Ambassador to the United States, one of the men who lied to Roosevelt's people as the Japanese were about to bomb Pearl Harbor.

We were silent for a while, suffering. It was very hot, but we both shivered from the loss of blood. I could not remember this island's name. I could not recall my sister's face. She would be all my parents have left. It was not amazing that they let me join the army. They could so easily have ended this ridiculous venture. My father must have understood I would die before thirty. Why not do it defending my country?

Sam snored in a strange way, and I saw he was breathing bubbles of blood out his nostrils. I considered waking him. Why not let him die quietly? But I wouldn't want to miss even these last awful minutes of life. I shook him. He woke with a start. His grip on his rifle made me think he might shoot me. He came to and remembered who I was. "Sorry," he said. "I was dreaming of that girl, Michiko. She gave herself to me one night, consolation for her snobbery maybe. I think I was rough with her. I had experience with prostitutes, and I could tell she was a virgin. Have you made love to a woman, Tom?" I said no. I imagined, without knowing why, that Sam was at this moment a fuller receptacle of his shrinking personality than I was. He was silent, and I lay on my side, not looking at him. I rolled over to hear the rest of this story, but he had died. His eyes were open. They had small pocks in them, like a golf ball.

I believe I died very soon after that, but time was strange those last moments. It may have taken an hour. I continued talking with Sam. I told the story of my uncle, who lived on some land near Southampton. In the summer he worked farms, day labor. He retreated to this shack outside Southampton in the winter. He had a dog and a shotgun. Every morning, in his later years, he fired the shotgun in the air, to let his nearest neighbor know he was still alive. One morning he didn't fire the shotgun.

I loved the way my mind felt—intensely focused, alert, transfixed—as I worked through this problem of dying. It was very much like working on a poem, but without the maddening, delightful, emotionally charged imprecision of words. My sister would find me in my room, at my desk, not writing, but pondering some particular problem, and she would complain that I loved my sadness, that I seemed to revel in melancholy. I suppose this was true. I had not expected to return from this war alive. I was not yet an accomplished poet. I was young, still growing. If I had not volunteered for this war I might have become a good poet, but I also have the feeling I would have been a modeler, someone who saw other people's structures and strategies and imitated them beautifully, without really finding his own unique way. When I solved this problem of dying, it was as though my body, which moments ago had been a large complicated knot, was untied with a single firm tug. Then my body seemed to buzz, tapping into a low galvanic current. Then the current was switched off.

I would ride my bike seven miles to the Green Street Café in Northampton, where I worked as a chef, and then seven miles home to my boyfriend, Jimmy, and our previous apartment in Easthampton, down the street from the wonderful old Majestic Theater, sadly no longer a house of porn. The family worried about the dark roads and late hours, but I said it was good exercise and kept my T-cell count up. I would ride into town on Route 10, which in Northampton becomes South Street, and then I would cross the Mill River, which used to run through the center of Northampton, before the Army Corps of Engineers rerouted it south and east to prevent flooding downtown. I would pass the South Street Grade School, my first school, and the college-owned apartment my parents rented on Fort Hill when we arrived in Northampton in 1962. I would turn left through the parking lot and grounds of Hawley Junior High School. I would dismount the bike and walk it up a small steep hill to the Forbes Library parking area, and then I would ride around to West Street and take a crosswalk to Green Street, directly across from Smith College, where my father taught for thirty years.

Now, these last months of my life, I stay in, watching horror movies and pornography and the weather channel. Jimmy dresses up as Cleopatra in a miniskirt to do housework, takes a few odd jobs around the area, and brings home stray boyfriends from clubs in Holyoke and Northampton. I do not complain of this behavior. Jimmy and I have each lost a previous boyfriend to AIDS. It is a way of honoring me—bringing home for my approval possible future mates.

Alec Baldwin and Nicole Kidman's movie *Malice* begins with a college student leaving College Hall at "Westerly College," which is actually Smith College, whose campus and adjacent town were used as the film's location. The student is about to be raped and badly beaten up in her Victorian house off campus, and she rides her bike home. She leaves the campus and passes along familiar (to me) shops on Main Street, then turns left on Center Street, all of which makes geographical sense. In the next shot she's back on Main Street downtown, riding under the railroad bridge toward Hadley and Amherst, which makes no sense. Then illogically she's gliding past the Smith College chapel on Elm Street, which is on the other side of town from the railroad bridge and she's heading in the opposite direction. Finally, she turns onto a side street across from the one I grew up on, and she enters a house that would not be rented to college students.

I like the way the film operates, cutting and pasting location shots with no regard for geography or logical progression through space, working more like the way a dream does. The opening of *Who's Afraid of Virginia Woolf?* also chooses a number of interesting moody shots of the Smith College campus and stitches them together to make it seem like Elizabeth Taylor and Richard Burton are walking across campus. *Malice* is a good *bad* movie, built on bizarre logic, almost a spoof of gothic horror. The plot of the serial rapist in a college town is a red herring for the real story, which is about medical insurance fraud. The film doesn't use horror movie music to set up the opening scene. Northampton is too pretty and maybe too green to menace us. The central plot of the movie, that Nicole Kidman has married associate dean Bill Pullman and then has slowly given herself a serious cyst on an ovary (don't ask how), in order to collude with the surgeon, her longtime lover, Alec Baldwin, on a massive malpractice settlement against him. Baldwin has just shown up in town and turns out to be an old high school classmate of Pullman's. I returned home a little over a year ago, after fifteen years in New York. "I came home to die," I like to tell unsuspecting strangers. My dreams have an aimlessness similar to *Malice*'s opening. I lived in New York, and I let my driver's license lapse, so I've driven only occasionally here in Northampton recently. My dreamscapes are those of a walker. A stretch of the Mill River where Doug and I used to stroll. Center Street to go to the apartment of an Edwards Church assistant minister who desperately wanted to seduce me but didn't know how to. The Three County Fairgrounds, which strangely was the fevered high point of my early adolescence—the moral release of a kind of circus in town.

One of the last times I felt up to going out for an afternoon with Jimmy (not even a night on the town), he took me to Pearl Street, a bar that fancies itself a New York club. There are a handful of gay bars in Northampton and Amherst, but I asked to go to this straight hangout. Jimmy was irritated by the choice, but he was also indulgent. We had Long Island Iced Teas, his craze that month. The bar has a large-screen TV going at all times, day and night. The images on the screen are of Northampton, from a car driving through town shooting stock footage. There is a soundtrack of sorts, bad new pop, decent old rock standards, cued to the places whenever possible. This loop of film is about thirty minutes long, but it feels like you're in a large vehicle driving endlessly around town. The effect is mesmerizing for me, though not for Jimmy. When I sat at the same table with my sister, a year ago, she did not pay it much mind, either, even when I asked her to identify this locale or that one—she's lived here on and off all her life. For Barb, Northampton is second nature. The filmed town gives the college students and twenty-somethings who've stayed on in town the feeling of having not only a movie soundtrack for their lives but filmed images. Jimmy doesn't understand why I'm crying. I watch the video go from the Calvin Theater up King Street and then left onto Summer Street, and right onto Prospect, past our new temporary home on Winter Street. Or Jimmy misinterprets my tears. He is good with direct emotion, about AIDS, about the indignities we've gotten accustomed to. He gets frustrated when I overintellectualize, as I'm doing now. So I decide to let him comfort me for what he thinks I'm so sad about.

OCTOBER 1942
GARY O'DEA, 23
DEATH IN EGYPT

The day I got my draft notice my pimples disappeared. I like to clip my toenails so close it hurts to walk for a day or two, and this has been the case since morning. The first hour after my jeep crashed I could hear the tank battle still raging across the Qattara Depression. Thumps, thuds, and the shrill whine of mortars, because of poorly cleaned cannon barrels. This distant noise of war was reassuring. The silence that followed made me start digging my own grave. I know I won't be missed. I am an American lieutenant attached to Field Marshal Montgomery's command. They sent me on a reconnaissance mission to get me out of the way during this second major tank battle of the last four months. Montgomery's staff treated the two Americans assigned to his command better than Montgomery did, but we were, at best, ignored. We were there to observe strategy and report to the American command, for the day when the US joined the fighting in North Africa. I dug my grave with whatever wreckage from the jeep I could find. The best tool was a curved piece of windshield. What do the British call it? Windscreen.

For eons, hungry or suspicious cavemen, frustrated and jealous lovers, violent criminals, and, more recently, industrial machinery and automobiles have inflicted serious injury on the human body and soul, neither of which is adapted to cope with the stress. But warfare has always been the most pertinent stimulus for the management of vascular injuries. This is the curse of a photographic memory. Last night I was reading a textbook on surgery the field marshal's private doctor had loaned me. I was driving at the edge of some deep valley southwest of the battle. I was doing a bit of sightseeing in the midst of war—it was difficult to keep the vehicle away from the dramatic views, the sea of bright yellow reeds three hundred feet below and two miles away. The jeep hit a patch of sand on a gentle slope, and I looked on helplessly, as if this took minutes to happen. The earth did a series of gyrations. I rolled with the jeep, then without it, but the peculiar consciousness of an accident like this slows time. I'm sure nothing penetrated my body. I was watching, lazily, as if from a daybed. No bones broken, no tendons snapped. I stood up, uninjured, blessing my good luck, happy to be alive.

Despite my conviction that no piece of the jeep had broken skin, I took a moment to gather my senses, and I noted a deep wound on my left side, wetness and a throbbing, as well as dizziness when I raised my arms above my head to wave pathetically at tanks two miles away. Montgomery chose this narrowest spot between the Qattara Depression and the Mediterranean to defend Egypt and the Middle East from Rommel.

War depends on good maps. The canyon drops steeply from here. No tanks will come anywhere near me, because the sand and hidden cliffs mask great danger even in the broad daylight. This is what I was sent to find out, and it found me.

Our Indians have brought in one of Philip's men: his name is Cherauckson, a man of about twenty years, who says he lost his company, admits he fought against the English at the swamp bridge. He was with thirty men who went to get corn out of their barns when the English shot down four of them, but he escaped. All our Indians say he is one that killed English. Indeed he did own it and then denied it and since denies everything. His shoes are hog skin with the hair on, his stockings linsey-woolsey, his breeches are bed ticking, his coat an English coat. Our Indians have suffered a great deal of pain to get him to confess, but he says little. He will not say what English are killed nor what Indians, only that Philip has forty men left and is gone he knows not where. This Indian Cherauckson has been wandering in the woods these eleven days and lived upon deer he killed. He had some venison in his stockings. A Windsor Indian woman was out a little from the fort, and he approached her. She brought him in to our Indians, who bound him and brought him to me. All the Indians desired he be killed, so I bid two of our men to take him out and shoot him, which was done accordingly. The Lord grant that all our enemies may perish so.

October 1942
Gary O'Dea, 23
Death in Egypt

Save waste fats for explosives. Take them to your meat dealer. When you ride alone you ride with Hitler. The wound still thrums, but ominously the bleeding has stopped. The wound that bleeds does not kill. I am writing with my left hand, if the handwriting seems a bit awkward (because my right side is growing lazy). Long ago, Father injured my throwing arm—I played third base on the high school team, not bad, but lots of room for improvement. I was trying to intervene in a "private discussion" he was having with Mother. So I taught myself to be ambidextrous. It is October 24, 1942.

This hot air takes me back to last summer in Northampton, Massachusetts, my hometown. Old man Warner's pond. You bike well past his house, acting like you're not even thinking of going to the pond. Then, casually, as if to adjust the chain that's always falling off, you dismount and quick dart into the thicket. You lean the bike against the tree where someone engraved, "GO," and you break a new trail through poison oak, ferns, elm, and blackberry bushes. Every year, New England stuns you with its jungle growth, after the arid empty winter months. The pond is a mile from the road. Between the road and the pond is the bog. You avoid the bog at all costs, even in favor of a certain patch of blackberry bushes that hides a ravine so expertly you've fallen into it three times. I enjoyed swimming alone most, but the first time I took Martha with me, she fell in love with the spot and she insisted we go there every chance we got.

I am Gary O'Dea, of Market Street, just off the graveyard that Bridge Street borders on the other side. At this very moment, in Northampton, it is snowing—somehow I know this is true—the kind of wet March stuff we sometimes get in January, and my sister is out shoveling. She knows I prefer she wait. The pattern of freshly fallen snow on our walk, after the storm has finished, is exquisite. I like to be the first to walk in snow, and the graveyard across the road gives me ample opportunity for that sport.

What can one do to make dying easier? My father left home when I was fifteen, a relief to the family despite the great shame of it. Martha can barely receive me in her mouth. I am surprised by the sensation. She says she's good at it. She suggested this method, even though we had done it the correct way several times. I was shocked by the proposition, but a boy does not question these things. She said she'd get pregnant otherwise, and besides she wanted me to have a lot of different memories of her. She left unsaid, *in case I die*. But why should I need memories of her? Shouldn't it be the other way around? I laugh at the thought: Martha was not very smart or pretty, despite that stunning body. But I'm no Adonis. After the pimples cleared up, my face is still not what you would call handsome. Because of baseball, I have a few muscles. I am a poor Mick with too much brains and too little future, Coach always told me. I know what kind of catch I am—or was. Still, Martha was always kind. She went with other boys, but I felt privileged. I learned a great deal from her.

Mother, I apologize for these thoughts, but I want you to hear all of your son, not just the parts that would show me well to the world. I am writing in the ledger book you gave me, with all these irritating cross-hatching lines in red and blue. My brain is not functioning well. I won't apologize for the stories, because I am dying.

Every once in a while on the horizon I can see a tank or a jeep, but I doubt they can see the makeshift flag I made out of the exhaust pipe and a blanket I was carrying along in case I wanted to picnic (my own lunacy: a picnic on the edge of a great tank battle). Weakness. Give me a moment.

In boot camp, we heard the news that a fellow in the platoon that trained just before us was the first American soldier killed in North Africa. My bunkmate Myzorski said to a roomful of scared GIs, "Speaking of dying, I'm dying for a cigarette. Anybody got one?" The drill instructor laughed so hard we thought he'd burst a blood vessel. But he also rode Myzorski mercilessly from that point on. What will I be? The fourth or fifth American killed. Not much glamour in that.

My older brother was always there, always talking in perfect rounded sentences as a child. He explained the world to me for several years in which I enjoyed having it explained to me and then for many years after, in which I did not. Geoffrey was my model of the thinker. He read and debated and thought, so I did none of these things—I played sports, dreamed of an athletic career, would not read a book for pleasure until I was sixteen. Geoff was thought and I was motion. Later, Geoffrey became motion—sex and cooking—he was a great chef. I became thought—writing and a cautious, deliberate approach to living and love. Before a date with a woman in New York in 1987, Geoff asked me, "Are you going to get laid?" I am deaf in one ear, so I misheard, "Are you going to be late?" meaning casually tardy, not overeager. I jumped into an earnest explanation of why I wouldn't be late because I did not like the politics of dating, and Geoffrey gave me a goofy, affectionate look, mystified by me, maybe perversely impressed by such sincerity. That same evening Geoff told me about sleeping with more than ten men at the Saint, a private gay dance and sex club on Second Avenue in the East Village. "Sleeping with?" I asked, while wondering if that actually involved ten orgasms, which sounded physically impossible or at least painful. "I chose the disinfected phrase for you," Geoff said.

OCTOBER 1942
GARY O'DEA, 23
DEATH IN EGYPT

The first night was much colder than I expected, or else I'm losing blood internally and just feeling cold. Still, the desert temperature drops dramatically at nightfall. Night comes quickly here, so much closer to the equator. One thinks mournfully of the long, languid sunsets of a June night. Or Martha walking naked off into the lilac-scented dark—the easy roll of her bottom, the breasts from behind just slivers of moons.

I grow weak, Mother.

Last night was bad. I think only one night passed. Woke with a bad taste. Slept fitfully. Small animals come closer and closer. I can see the glint of their yellow eyes. These are not coyotes or wolves, but I hear cheetahs roam the Depression. It is comforting to know that I will end as a meal.

I have already died a few times. It is a clean feeling. I am very still, head on the sand. Then a great drop in air pressure, and I am rolling as if on some kind of solid surf. In a sort of dream I find myself opening up at Harlow & Fennessey's stationer at six, before school. A gorgeous spring day, trees that light green, and I pick up the bundles of newspapers from Holyoke and Springfield to take them inside. An old Ford drives down Masonic Street. I'm not sure, but it might be Father. Stubble, eyes glazed over as always, hand twitching on the wheel. This is the first time I caught sight of Martha, leaving her mother's house for her job before school, at Ann August's dress shop. In her light flowery dress, with the sun in front of her, she looks naked. A stunning view, but I am troubled by sharing it with my father, who does not appear to see me standing five feet away on the pavement. He is not driving by my place of employment on purpose to spy on me—because he can't know I work there. It is a mere accident, and it implicates him in my lust, whatever sweet outcome there is later with Martha.

I had hoped to outlive Father. What keeps me alive each night is the thought that I don't know whether he is alive or dead. I hesitate to hope for his death, although my rational mind tells me I may only be hoping for something that has already happened, so it is not a sin. If he's alive, this more and more independent mind tells me I am just giving in to contrary-to-fact thinking.

Also buried in the Bridge Street cemetery: Caleb Strong (1745–1819), Isaac Chapman Bates (1779–1845), Elijah Hunt Mills (1776–1829), Esther White (1721–1821), Eli Porter Ashmun (1770–1819), Charles Delano (1820–1883), and Osmyn Baker (1800–1875). My memory for particulars grows stronger the closer to death I inch. I researched this one beautiful fall afternoon, kicking leaves from gravestones. The shallow grave I dug is my bed.

Tanks have stopped patrolling the visible horizon. I can no longer sit. I lose the strength to pen these

I am no longer I. He lifts a palm He breathes

All my worldly go to

July 1678
Cornet Joseph Parsons, 60

I lived a complicated life before we moved our homestead to Northampton. We were among the first settlers in 1654. My bride, the former Mary Bliss, disliked this valley whose way south was blocked by mountains that went against God's wishes, ranging east to west, rather than north to south. I bought land, sat on court, built the first meeting house, buried the first pastor, and fought neighbors who made suit against my wealth. I forgave all, even those who accused my wife of witchcraft. The nine months she spent in a Boston jail improved her—she returned slimmer, more open to sensation and God's will, a sound sleeper, acquitted of all crimes. Some of the commerce I traded in: fox skin, nottamag, musquash skin, wildcat, marten, woodshaw, moose skin, beaver testicles (for making musk), red shag cotton, pink penistone, blue duffield, Devonshire kersey, coronation tammy, black serge, holland linen, knives, scissors, awls, axes, mackhooks, and burning-glasses for lighting fire, as well as inkhorns, looking-glasses, ivory and bone combs, and gilt boxes in nests. I most enjoyed commerce with the Indians. I savored the greater wealth of friendship. The Indians gave me the mushrooms my wife cooked in fine stews. When she ate them raw she saw insects, birds, and mice on the ceiling. I put her to bed on these occasions and barred the door, but the witchery they accused her of turned out to be sleepwalking, a crime that harmed nothing but sleep. One day I rode west into the hills with a half-Dutch, half-Indian man. We bargained with a ratty conference of Indians. This distressing crew did not dampen my spirits. I listened to them read the landscape— making plain how they used the forests as a sort of large farm, carefully burning the undergrowth twice a year so game would be easy to hunt. The skinny traders huddled together for warmth. I wanted to join their flimsy union, but my interpreter suggested they suffered from the pox. Their eyes were wet and yellow. I saw in them an understanding of the land that made me yearn to translate and enrapture their souls to mine.

DECEMBER 1993
MURRAY KITELEY, 63

I was watching a rerun of the television show *Cheers* on a hospital bed next to the bed my son lay dying on. The bartender Coach hears a ringing phone, looks around briefly, then picks up the phone from under the bar and answers, "Cheers"— the name of the bar in the television show. He listens for a moment, then speaks to the bar, "Is there an Ernie Pantuso in the room?" A guy at the bar says, "Coach, *you're* Ernie Pantuso." For all of that first season, we only knew this one name, Coach. Coach looks surprised, then he picks up the phone and says, "Ernie Pantuso here." I laughed at this, swelled with several other emotions, heard the canned laughter from the television set, felt it wash over me, heard on a lower level my son's labored breathing like a machine climbing a set of stairs—the nurses had just given him another massive dose of morphine— enough, I knew, to still the strong heart, but not yet, not now. I laughed, and in the curious intensity of the moment heard my laugh double back on me, replay itself several times, so that it was possible I might be embarrassed by it as one is alarmed by one's own voice on a tape recorder, but I was not embarrassed. I saw the laugh's colors. Green, brown, brownish-green, red, blood red—my son had been hemorrhaging all morning. Then I no longer heard any sounds. I wondered if I'd shifted onto the remote and shut off the TV's volume, but it lay there feet away, and I watched the characters on the screen talk, howl, whisper, giggle, without any sound. I switched channels to the end credits of a movie Geoff had been watching regularly for the last few weeks. Something about a groundhog. Nat King Cole was singing:

> What a day this has been
> What a rare mood I'm in
> Why it's almost like being in love.
> There's a smile on my face
> For the whole human race.
> I swear I was falling
> Swear I was fallin';
> Well, it's almost like being in love.

I lie flat, I lift myself, raise my eyes, my ears, to gray skies, film
at left, lot for sale, my Mom sometimes. It feels as if I'm ill,
last rites far off, airy talk of relief. A film tells its tale, reiterates,
retells. See it later, time after time. My gills leak some jelly. My
farts smell like a trail to some afterlife. A memory: I oil a steak
for a roast. Flames eat at a grill. I make a last meal for my jailer,
my male-female, Jimmy. After salt, after sesame aioli, a fair fate
for a gay meal like steak satay is fire. Flames still eat at a grill,
eat time, regale my family, Jimmy. A memory of some eatery: I
forget, a small item like risotto, or more like a rissole? I forget a
lot lately. I lie flat, leak from my gills, a lake forms at my feet. A
glossary of memories: leeks, yams, milk fat, lots of fat, a rioja
or a merlot, oysters frittata, Gramma Elsie's tarts, steak tartar,
key lime fly off meager flakes of my gray matter. A femmy
memory: Jimmy meets James at a small eel store, stammers
amors. Jimmy asks if I'll say okay. I say okay. My flame left

me for a less-fragile male. I'm all ears, all eyes, all self, selfless, listless, Geoffless. Mortality, remorse, mortgage, my last room. I am a memory, some aroma time forgot after a life of great meals. I lie flat, list left, I die.

Here is the girl's head like an exhumed gourd. Oval-faced, prune-skinned. We unswaddle the wet fern of her hair and make an exhibition of its coil, let air at her leathery beauty. Vinland is cruel. We have found this body in the bog by the lake, beheaded, the stone blade lovingly laid by the severed neck. Who were these people? Along this great north-south lake, a bread-loaf mountain our benchmark. We elect one among us to suffer for the ancient murder of this girl. He does not protest during the long hike back to the ocean. He speaks wistfully of the days when there was no frost in winter. We thought we'd found paradise. We were but tricked. Winters are now as bad here as they are in Greenland. The condemned man finally tires of the weight of his canoe on the second of three days and cries out at the cruelty of this punishment *before* being put to death. Someone says, "But you don't have to walk all the way back to camp." We tie him into his canoe. He will be able to see only sky. He floats out to sea but hits a sand bar. We watch until the sun goes down, and at sunrise his canoe is gone. He will die of lack of water on water. God is cold.

I sit comfortably slouched in the old Volvo, my dress billowing over me like a topsail. My boyfriend of five months drives along Interstate 91, over familiar landscape. I have not visited my hometown in ten years. My grandmother took me in (but not the twins) when I was nine, after my parents died. Uncle Frank put Grandma in a rest home a few years ago because of Alzheimer's. My boyfriend, John Gathers, arranged this research trip for himself to study the archives of Northampton's 200-year-old newspaper. He's writing a book about the town. John also grew up in Northampton, but we'd met only once, despite having been born two days apart, at Cooley Dickinson Hospital.

It is dark by the time we glide past the Oxbow, now a tame little lake for recreation, not the beautiful bend in the river Thomas Cole painted in the 1830s. John drives carefully, reaching over every once in a while to cup my breast through the soft fabric of the summer dress. He tells me everything north of the gap between Mt. Tom and Mt. Holyoke was a lake, as far as Canada, a thousand years ago. I tell him it was more like ten thousand years ago. He keeps his eyes reassuringly on the road, but I can see the lust in them anyway. We stay on the interstate until just past Northampton, and then we take the Hatfield exit. We drive down Route 10 to a motel in the woods where we have reservations. He pulls into the parking lot and jumps out to register. I stay in the car—it is a beautiful early August night, the sumacs beginning to redden, the smell of pond water and pine intermingling. He returns quickly. He's good at things like this. He drives to the room around back. No other cars, no lights on in any of the motel room windows. I step out of the car. He comes around from the driver's side of the car, and his long hungry gaze makes me fidget.

We walk into the woods without talking. We arrive at a chain link fence. While my back is turned he takes off his clothes. So I slip out of my dress—I have nothing on under it. We are doing this all the time, wherever we can do it safely. I see the lights of a building through the trees, but they are a good distance off. This is a private sanctuary. John takes my fingers and gently twines them in the fencing. He presses up against my back, his breath on my neck, in my hair.

The aroma of recently cut grass takes me back to a time that still causes serene sadness—those weeks and months after my mother died. The intense pleasure dissipates the melancholy somewhat, but not completely. My boyfriend is inside me, but he is also not there.

I feel sure he is making me pregnant. I can tell I'm ovulating, by my heightened sense of smell and touch. We agreed, from the beginning, that we would have a baby as soon as we could. I try to will the sperm into the egg.

We pull apart.

In one motion I throw the dress over my head and slip inside it. John says, with a catch in his voice, "That was beautiful—the way you just melted into your dress." He slouches against the chain link fence. He radiates calm. I lean into his shoulder. Rain begins to fall—warm, soft rain that brings out a fragrance in the woods like freshly baked bread. Somewhere nearby issues a scratchy recording of a bugle playing "Taps," which is both creepy and moving. Life is not simply story, but chemistry, physics, and behavior, layered over biology in a beautiful synergy.

I have often used (and burnished) other people's words—sometimes the words of historical figures, sometimes someone else's completely unrelated words when they fit the moment I was pondering. Characters whose last names are Kiteley are portraits of my own family—myself, my brother, sister, mother, father, and grandparents. In many ways these are the most fictionalized narratives in the book, although the details that underpin these characters are accurate (or at least faithful to my own or other family members' memory of events). Historical figures, especially those whose recorded utterances I've used, are as historically accurate as I could make them, although much of the presentation of these ghosts is also necessarily phantasmagoric. I played with the following texts (preceded by the month and the year they appear in the book) in various ways, paraphrasing, quoting directly for a few sentences, or rewriting as I saw fit:

January 1062: Seamus Heaney, "Strange Fruit," in *North*; May 1654: William Miller, *A New History of the United States*; February 1680: Richard Slotkin, *Regeneration Through Violence*; and Mike Weaver, *William Carlos Williams: The American Background*; October 1727: Elizabeth Dodd, *Marriage to a Difficult Man*; December 1826: *The Boston Globe*, January 29, 1990; November 1852: Olive Gilbert, *The Narrative of Sojourner Truth*; and Hope Hale Davis, "Northampton Association of Education and Industry," in *The Northampton Book: Chapters from 300 Years in the Life of a New England Town*; March 1930: Laura Mullen, *The Tales of Horror*; December 1943: T. S.

Eliot, *Four Quartets*; Randall Jarrell, "The Death of the Ball Turret Gunner"; June 1944: William Vollmann, *The Rainbow Stories*; July 1958: Sylvia Plath, *The Unabridged Journals*; April 1989: Alice Ambrose and Morris Lazerowitz, *Ludwig Wittgenstein: Philosophy and Language*.

I would like to thank Brian Evenson, Brenda Mills, Eli Gottlieb, Robert Urquhart, Jennifer Pap, Rikki Ducornet, Joanna Howard, Selah Saterstrom, Eric Melbye, Laura Mullen, Cole Swensen, Ralph Berry, Clifford Chase, Allen Hibbard, Bin and Linda Ramke, Jan Gorak, Michael Gorra, Edward Shanahan, Wayne Dodd, Mark Tursi, my sister Barbara Hill and her husband Pete Hill, my wife Cynthia Coburn, and my parents, Murray and Jean Kiteley. I am also grateful to all my friends who welcomed the postcard stories, which make up a good part of this book.